Dare to Dream

Vera Berry Burrows

A Wings ePress, Inc.
Mainstream Novel

Wings ePress, Inc.

Edited by: Jeanne Smith
Copy Edited by: Heather O'Connor
Executive Editor: Jeanne Smith
Cover Artist: Trisha FitzGerald

All rights reserved

Wings ePress Books
www.wingsepress.com

Copyright © 20xx by: Author
ISBN 978-1-61309-667-3

Published In the United States Of America

Wings ePress Inc.
3000 N. Rock Road
Newton, KS 67114

Dedication

To Alan who brings sunshine into my life and gives me loving support in all that I do.

* * *

One

Anne Marie O'Shea was left on the doorstep of St Anthony's orphanage on the twenty-first of June 1944. The label attached to her jacket said she was two years old. Her little face was stained with tears and contorted by crying. When the enormous, carved wooden doors opened, she was lifted from the doorstep into the arms of a lady in long black robes and whose wire-rimmed glasses were perched on the end of her nose.

"Now who have we got here?" Sister Agatha asked as she picked up the tiny form. "Shhh, my darlin'. You are safe now." The child clung to the lady. "That's a good girl. All those tears are making you look like the devil himself! There, there. Come on now. We'll take you to the Reverend Mother. She'll know what to do."

"The child will have to be cleaned up and placed with another girl...maybe Bella Jones. She's nearly five years old and should be given some responsibility. To be sure she's in need of something to steer her away from her wilful ways," the Reverend Mother advised.

"I'm not so sure it will work, but if you think it will be the right move, we should give it a try," Sister Agatha said warily. "This package was attached to the child's coat belt, Mother. Shall we put it away until she is old enough to appreciate it?"

"I think we should, Sister," the Mother Superior agreed. "Put it in the safe with the other keepsakes we are holding in trust."

And so Bella and Anne Marie were placed together in the dormitory with twenty-two other girls, none more than five years old, whose eyes stared blankly at yet another new girl in their midst.

Bella looked round at the girls who were sitting on their beds and they stared back. "This is my friend, Annie, and don't any of youse think about taking her off me, 'cos if you do, I'll give you the biggest punch on the nose you've ever had in your life." She glared at them and then whispering, she said, "Come on, Annie. I'll show you where we can hide from Sister Aggie, 'cos I'm four, nearly five and I'm older than you."

~ * ~

A few weeks later, after lessons, she grabbed Annie's hand and dragged her out of the dorm, down a long corridor to the back door of the convent. "Don't move, Annie, and keep quiet." On tiptoe and stretching herself as high as she was able, she reached the latch and opened the door. Annie stood still and watched Bella as she looked around to see if any of the nuns was watching. Finding that they were alone, she took Annie's hand again and pulled her through the doorway. Skulking round the rear wall of the building, the two little girls made their way into the vegetable garden and ran as fast as they could to the gap in the hedge at the far end. Once there, Bella pulled Annie down onto her knees and together they crawled behind the hedge to the biggest of the trees where windfall apples lay in abundance on the ground.

"Eat!" Bella instructed.

Annie obeyed and took a bite of the green apple in her hand. "Ugh," she complained.

"Eat it!" Bella told her again. "Don't be a softy. It'll make you grow big like me."

Annie stared at the apple in her hand, shook her head vigorously at Bella and dropped the apple on the ground.

"Please yourself," Bella said dismissively. "Don't cry when they don't give you enough to eat at dinner." She continued to eat her apple and then another before she was ready to sneak back into the house.

In bed that night, Annie heard Bella crying and, in her own loneliness, she wept with her new friend until she fell asleep. When she awoke the next morning, Sister Agatha was changing Bella's bed and Bella was nowhere to be seen.

"Bella?" she whimpered. "Bella?" and tears rolled down her cheeks.

"Oh, don't cry, little Annie. Bella has gone to take a bath. I don't know what she'd been eating, but she made an awful mess in her bed. She's the devil's daughter at times that one. The mischievous wee soul always has an agenda alien to ours. May the good Lord help us all!"

Gradually, Annie settled in and clung to Bella whatever they were doing. "You'll be okay with me, Annie," Bella told her.

"Okay," Annie repeated. "Wuv you, Bella."

"Don't say that word, Annie," the four, almost five-year-old snapped. Annie stared at Bella with wide eyes. Bella continued, quietly for once and with far too much sadness for one of such tender years. "Nobody loves us."

Only once had the Mother Superior introduced them to a couple looking to adopt. They only wanted one child and the Reverend Mother had not wanted to separate Bella from Annie nor vice versa. "I have to insist these little girls stay together. They are good for each other and I doubt they would be happy if they were separated. I'm sorry, Mr and Mrs Blackshaw. Perhaps we might introduce you to little Renee. She's sweet and..."

Mr and Mrs Blackshaw had indeed met Renee and decided to love her as their own.

~ * ~

When Annie was ten years old, Bella showed her a shady nook she had discovered in the garden and in her own inimitable way, she scared off the other children if they dared to venture within fifty yards of her den. One Sunday afternoon, after Mass and after lunch, she and Annie sat in the den shaded from the unfamiliar hot June sun and hidden from the rest of the children and nuns. "You can be my sister,

Annie," she said. "If we prick our fingers on a rose thorn and mix our blood, that'll make us real sisters."

"But you have brown skin and black hair and I have white skin and fair hair," Annie told her.

"I'm only brown because my birth mother was Italian. Sister Agatha blurted it out once when she was telling me off about something."

"But you are always getting told off, Bella."

I know," Bella admitted. "I only do naughty things when I'm bored. It would be too boring in here if we didn't misbehave occasionally."

"Occasionally?" Annie couldn't help smirking.

"Well, anyway, just let me tell you." Bella said, eager to finish her explanation. "Sister Agatha was telling me off because I was kicking up about something—I can't remember what—but she said…" Bella mimicked Sister Agatha's Irish accent. *"I don't want to see that Latin paddy anymore, Bella Jones. You allow your Italian blood to boil over too often to be sure.* When I asked her what a Latin paddy was, she said it was the blood I'd got from my Italian mother, whoever she was. Well, Italian or not, she obviously didn't want me if she gave me to the nuns to raise." She went momentarily quiet and Annie noticed that her friend was clearly moved by the significance of her past.

The years went by seemingly slowly at times and Bella instigated numerous rule- breaking pranks such as pinching food from the kitchen when everybody was asleep; placing drawing pins on the teacher nun's chair; hiding the chalkboard duster in the classroom and stealing the nuns' underwear from the laundry to hang on the wrought iron gates at the front of the convent. Annie learned quickly that rules were actually meant to be obeyed, not broken. As the two girls grew, both physically and academically, they remained close and loyal to each other at all times. In spite of their evolving different views of the insular world around them, they were never far apart and Annie learned to accept without animosity that it was just the way Bella was made and she was willing to accept it. By the time Annie was a teenager, she began to wonder what life was like outside the confinements of the orphanage. *Oh that I could be like the butterfly in my dreams,* she thought. *The one that flies away to escape the fiercely domineering bumble bee.* She sighed. *Unfortunately, I wake up before I find out where the butterfly goes and can never pick up the dream where I left off.*

~ * ~

1957

"What we need is a bit of magic in our lives," Annie announced dreamily as she looked around at the girls who had chosen to stay indoors and do some knitting since it was wet and windy outside. It was Sunday and after Mass they were allowed free time to stroll around the grounds outside or to knit baby bootees ..."For the poor wee girls who have become with child far too early in their lives," Sister Agatha explained every time she handed out the needles and wool.

"Magic? Magic? I don't believe in magic," Bella stated caustically. "Fate, perhaps, but not magic. For goodness sake, Annie, grow up. You can't honestly think that by waving a magic wand, all your troubles will disappear."

"I'm not talking about magicians, or conjurors, or whatever you want to call them. I'm talking about the unexplainable things that happen in your life. It hasn't happened to us yet, but I still believe that there's a magical moment for everyone. Everybody deserves one of those," Annie explained, her ardour not dampened by Bella's disinterest and then more quietly she said, "Why are you always so negative, Bella? Surely now that we've grown up a lot, we are allowed to dream a little."

"Dreamers live in a fantasy world, Annie, not the real world. We have to survive. We were put on this earth to scratch and scrape a living. We don't even know where we came from and who cares? I'll tell you who...nobody. I'm seventeen years old; you are fifteen, at least we think we are. How could we possibly know? It's time you came down to earth, girlie. Accept your lot with good grace," Bella urged. "Don't chase after the impossible."

That night, Annie looked round the austere dormitory, cringing at her friend's withering look as she had delivered those scathing comments. *I just wish something good would happen,* she thought, her mind full of the dreams she had secretly nurtured for as long as

5

she could remember. She stared through the darkness at the damp patches on the ceiling, the worn carpet on the floor and the rickety bed upon which she tried to sleep each night. "Does it always have to be like this?" she whispered to herself. She shivered as she pulled the thin bedspread up to her chin.

Annie had grown up in that building, but it was a place she refused to call home. According to Lily James, who had lived in a proper home with proper parents, homes were places where everybody was content and loving. Calling the orphanage home would be like admitting she was completely happy there and she couldn't in all honesty say that she had ever experienced happiness, as far as she knew. Perhaps she'd been content, but never truly happy. Her thoughts, although humble, were critical of what she had and did not have. *I suppose I should be happy to be alive. There's not much else to be happy about in this place. Oh, the nuns are all right, most of them, but I would love to live ... really live without having to ask permission to do everything.* She looked around again. *I'd paint this place, for one thing, and buy a new carpet.*

The miserable, dank surroundings did nothing to lift her spirits and her housemates too appeared to merely exist without hope or ambition. Few, if any, of those around her had rarely smiled with pleasure, let alone giggled merrily. She often wondered what it would be like to feel her belly jiggle with laughter, or have her sides ache through laughing too much. She had witnessed Alice Bowden laughing hysterically one night and she seemed to be in agony. She was taken away and never seen again, so Annie wasn't sure what that sort of laughing was all about or what had happened to Alice Bowden.

During all those years, the nearest Annie had come to laughing was a snigger when the dormitory sergeant had tripped over somebody's shoes as she inspected the dorm one morning. Annie hadn't dared to laugh, because the consequences would have been too unbearable. She bit her lip and held her breath, but there was a hint inside her stomach of what it might be like to laugh out loud. Yet the analysis in her head was contradictory. *It felt like a retch, but a pleasant one. Surely laughing and being happy don't make you feel sick.*

Bella was Annie's only close friend there. Together they had survived their years in the Catholic-run orphanage until Annie was over sixteen years old and deemed capable of living on her own.

"Bella," she said to her friend as they sat huddled in their den one cold and blustery Sunday afternoon. "Do you ever dream of a better life?"

Bella tutted. "No," she snapped. "How can people like us have a better life? We started off with nothing; we'll finish up with nothing."

"But even though we have nothing, we can dream," Annie told her.

"For pity's sake, Annie, stop dreaming about the impossible. Dreams are dreams. They never happen in real life. I give up with you. Face facts and don't ask for the moon." Bella was exasperated. "I know my place in life and it isn't mixing with the rich and famous."

"You're wrong, Bella. Don't ask me how I know, but I do. Something magical will happen for us, I just know it. Not just now, but sometime in our lives."

"I don't believe in magic either," Bella said. "I've told you hundreds of times before, it doesn't exist. Magicians, like the one Sister Geraldine brought in at Christmas when we were little kids, use tricks and sleight of hand. That's not magic; it's all one big con. And talking of cons, that magician was our Christmas present for that year! Don't talk to me ever again about magic, Annie. I don't want to hear it."

Annie fell silent. She pulled her coat round her and looked sadly at Bella who had turned her back on her.

"Come on, Annie," Bella said. "It's freezing out here. Let's go in where it's a bit warmer and..." she paused. "...next week we'll be leaving this place and I can't wait."

In April nineteen fifty-nine, they prepared to leave. Sister Agatha helped them with packing their few belongings in suitcases given to them by the Angels' Charity affiliated to the convent. "You know,' she said kindly, "You have to be grateful that the good Lord sent you to us. You have had a good education and you are leaving with the qualifications needed if you wish to continue your studies. There are colleges in and around Bolton…"

"Piff!" Bella spat. "How will we be able to live if we go into further education, Sister?"

Annie looked aghast. "Bella!" she said pointedly. "Watch your manners."

Sister Agatha smiled as she always did when Bella gave her opinion. "Come on now, Miss Bella," she said, "You have to acknowledge we have tried to help you on your way and Mrs Constable at Half Way House will guide you if you ask. She has links with the education authority. You have been very lucky that we allowed you, Bella, to stay on a couple of years extra so you and Annie could leave together. At least be pleased about that."

Bella rolled her eyes, but chose not to reply.

"And what about you, little Annie O'Shea?" Sister Agatha asked kindly.

Annie smiled a genuine smile that was easy when it was directed at Sister Agatha. "Oh, Sister, I'm nervous, but excited. Even though Bella thinks I'm silly, I dream of being successful at something. I'd like to be a nurse like Sister Augustina, but I'll see how things go. Thank you for all you have done for us."

"You just dare to dream, Annie," Sister Agatha encouraged. "Dare to dream."

Bella nudged Annie with a well directed elbow in her ribs and a glaring look to stop her from gushing further over Sister Agatha.

The astute nun smiled again. "Well, you should be on your way now," and she handed them each a leather purse.

Bella nodded as a gesture of appreciation. Annie said, "Thank you, Sister."

"The local education authority has issued grants for your board and lodging. That money will go direct to Mrs Constable, but there is money in your purses to keep you going for a while. Mrs Constable will be waiting at Half Way House. Take good care, both of you and good luck. God speed." She gave Annie a hug, but Bella was through the door before Sister Agatha could show her the same affection.

~ * ~

"Annie and Bella have left, Reverend Mother," Sister Agatha reported.

"Thank you, Sister. I do hope they succeed in life. I pray they will find whatever is God's will for them."

Sister Agatha nodded knowingly. "Bella Jones will bludgeon her way through life, I'm sure. Little Annie will think carefully before she acts."

"In spite of what Bella tells her to do," the Reverend Mother responded candidly. "Chalk and cheese they are, to be sure. I was very tempted to separate them on numerous occasions and yet Annie always stood her ground in a very quiet and delicate way. I really hoped that some of that child's humility would rub off on Bella." She smiled and shook her head slowly. "What will be, will be, Sister Agatha. God bless them both."

Two

The two girls stood outside the building that had been their resting place for most of their lives and they looked at each other, overwhelmed with feelings of independence thus far alien to them. Bella was the first to react. "Look at us, Annie. We're free! We are out on our own! No nuns to keep us in line. Today is the first day of the rest of our lives." She looked at Annie. "Oh for goodness sake, cheer up. Haven't we talked about what we'd do once we were on our own?"

"I know, Bella, but the thought of finding a job, one that will pay us enough money to do all those things we talked about and still leave us with enough money to pay for our keep, scares me to death! We have never had to worry about those things until now, have we?" Annie replied plaintively.

Both girls were still clutching the purses given to them by Sister Agatha as they left. Instinctively they looked down at the leather wallets and they opened them together. "Bloody hell!" Bella exclaimed.

"Oh my goodness gracious me," Annie whispered incredulously.

"There are fifty pounds here," Bella marvelled as she counted the five-pound notes in her hand. "Fifty pounds, Annie! Fifty pounds each! We're rich!"

"I have never seen a one-pound note, never mind five-pound notes. I'm overwhelmed," Annie rejoined. She looked down at the money in her hand and then back at the door several times. "Do you think we should go back in and say thank you?"

"No," Bella replied as she gave Annie a playful slap on the hand. "We already said thank you, didn't we? Come on, we'd best find Old Mother Constable. Fancy sending us to a place with a constable in charge," she continued and sniggered at her own little joke.

Half Way House was situated on Greenhough Lane at the edge of Rivington moor, between Rivington Pike and Winter Hill. It had once been the property of a cotton mill owner and upon his death, it had been bequeathed to the Angels' Charity. It was a very grand structure built of local sandstone in the Georgian style with four imposing pillars at the central front entrance and long sash windows on the ground and first floors. The attic rooms with dormer windows added a sort of glamour to the noble edifice and adorned the roof like a crown. Annie looked in awe at the magnificent facade of the old building.

"Look at that!" she enthused. "Who'd have thought we would ever live in such a place?"

Bella, ever the adversary of enthusiasm, threw a look of animosity towards Annie. "For pity's sake, Annie, it's still an institution. We'll still have rules and I wouldn't be surprised if the Constable woman is more hard-bitten than the nuns."

"Not all the nuns were hard-bitten, as you put it. Just a few were sticklers for the rules and you can't blame them for wanting to raise well-mannered and respectful young ladies before they turn them out into the world," she said as a retort to Bella's assessment of the situation. She stared at Bella and sighed. *I love Bella, but sometimes I don't like her. She's the nearest thing I have to a sister, but it is so obvious we are different, so very different.* She chose not to say anything further.

Bella grabbed Annie's arm and marched her to the door. She pulled on the doorbell and stood tall as they waited for the door to be opened.

"Do you think they have a butler?" Annie offered.

"Don't be stupid. It's a house for foundlings, not a stately home!" Bella cut in.

The door opened slowly and a round, ruddy, healthy-looking face peeped round it before Mrs Constable opened it fully to reveal herself. "Ah, you must be Annie and Bella. I was expecting you. Do come in," she greeted them amicably.

Neither girl said anything in reply and they followed Mrs Constable into the drawing room. It was luxuriously furnished with leather sofas and chintz curtains tied back with silk cord. The carpet was thick and patterned with a floral design and there was a thick wool rug in front of the marble fireplace in which flames of an open fire danced merrily. In the corner, by the window, a girl and a boy sat at a table, their heads bowed as they studiously wrote on exercise paper in loose-leaf folders. They glanced at the visitors and then without speaking, neither to Mrs Constable nor to each other, they got on with whatever they were doing.

"Come and sit by the fire. It's still a bit chilly outside for April, isn't it?" Mrs Constable invited.

Still quite speechless, Annie and Bella did as they were bid. Annie sat on the edge of the sofa, her hands nervously clasped on her knees. Bella leaned back, casually crossing her legs as she surveyed the opulence of the room and the welcoming atmosphere which contradicted her expectations. Her manner oozed confidence and Annie observed her friend's air that may have been considered impertinence.

Undeterred by Bella's display of arrogance, Mrs Constable continued. "I will show you to your rooms shortly, but first I must tell you what is allowed and what is not."

Bella looked pointedly at Annie and then at Mrs Constable. "I hope there aren't as many rules as there were at St Anthony's," she stated bluntly.

Annie was mortified and looked for Mrs Constable's reaction.

The comely woman was unperturbed. "You will understand, ladies, that when we have several guests living here at the same time, we must have rules in order that they are all comfortable together. I hope you will find our rules conducive to social niceties."

Bella rolled her eyes. Annie nodded prudently.

Mrs Constable continued undeterred. "You may come and go as you please so long as you let me know when you go out and when you return. There is a book in the entrance hall for you to sign out and sign in. You may have visitors in your rooms on Saturdays and Sundays between two o'clock in the afternoon and seven o'clock in the evening, but you must let me know how many and who they are so that I might provide refreshments if needed. Visitors may be here in the drawing room until nine o'clock. A bell is rung to let you know when it is time for them to leave. There is a laundry for you to wash your clothes and a clothes line in the garden to dry them. Irons and ironing boards are kept in the laundry. There are four of each and you should book them when you need them to avoid clashes of intentions at any particular time. I think that is all you need to know. Have you any questions?"

"Do we all eat together?" Bella asked. "You didn't mention that at all. I hope we don't have to buy our own food."

"No, Bella. Food is provided in the dining room and times are listed in your information leaflets in your rooms," Mrs Constable assured her. "You need not worry about that, Bella..." and then more deliberately, "... we are not here to starve you, but to nourish you in preparation for your lives in the big wide world. I hope you understand that."

Suitably chastised, a surly Bella did not reply.

"Welcome to Half Way House. I hope you will be happy here," Mrs Constable said cheerily. "Now I will show you to your rooms."

They climbed the impressive staircase in the entrance hall to the first floor. "This floor is Lower East where my quarters are and where the resident staff have their rooms. Above is Middle East and finally Upper East where the boys'rooms are," Mrs Constable explained. "Your rooms are on Middle East...ME3 and ME7."

"Aren't we together?" Annie asked.

Mrs Constable smiled. "No, you have your own room here. I know you are used to sharing, but it is usually every teenaged girl's dream to have her own room. I'm sure you will be happy with your own space, Annie."

"But she's always been with me," Bella interjected. "I'm not sure she'll settle on her..."

"I'll be fine, Bella," Annie interrupted.

"I don't know about that, Annie," Bella told her, but when Annie gave her a disdainful look, Bella was confused. *What's going on with Annie?* she thought. *She is suddenly being a little too bold. She's never spoken up for herself as long as I can remember. She's always relied on me to speak our minds. I'm not sure she'll settle in without me.*

~ * ~

Mrs Constable left the girls to settle in their rooms, rooms that were comfortably furnished and painted in pastel shades (Annie's was pale turquoise; Bella's shell pink) without being as opulent as the impressive reception rooms they had seen when they arrived. Each had a single bed against the wall to the right as they entered. The window, adorned with Jacquard curtains, was opposite the door and there was a window seat with cushions. To the left of the door was another door leading to a shower room with wash basin and toilet. Annie couldn't believe what she was seeing. The rest of the wall on the left was taken up with a double built-in wardrobe with one mirrored door, each unit separated with a dressing table, or desk depending on one's needs. A chair with a padded seat that matched the curtains was tucked under the dressing table and finally, in the corner by the bed was an upholstered armchair to match the curtains and cushions. Annie's eyes glistened with tears as she surveyed her own little home.

She opened her suitcase containing the few clothes she had accumulated during her time at St Anthony's. She had sufficient underwear for two weeks, several skirts and tops and a best dress and coat for Sundays. She had a pair of flat shoes for everyday use and her best shoes were her pride and joy because they were black patent leather with pointed toes and kitten heels. None of her clothes was new except for underwear and shoes, but she had looked after them and was proud of how she looked when she dressed up.

At the bottom of her suitcase was a small mother of pearl crucifix and a small dark red box she had never seen before. It was square and flat and had an ornate lid decorated with a delicate gold leaf pattern around the edges. Carefully, she opened it and a note fell out onto the floor. Finding a silver locket in the box, she gasped in awe as she bent to pick up the note. She looked in wonder at the beautiful piece of jewellery in her hand. It was about the size of a two shilling piece with gold heart in the centre and when the light from the window caught it, it twinkled like a star in the sky. Carefully, she opened the locket to reveal the photograph of a baby. *That must be me,* she conjectured and she unfolded the note which read: *To my baby girl, Anne Marie O'Shea. May she have the kind of life I could never give her. Thank you for looking after her. God bless her and God bless you.*

"My name is Anne Marie," she whispered, "and somebody, somewhere loved me." *Sister Agatha must have kept it for me until I was able to look after it myself. It was Bella who gave me the name Annie, after Little Orphan Annie, I suppose. Not very imaginative though, because Bella was only four then, yet I think I like the idea of it being a literary character if I might stretch the concept of a comic strip character that far.* She folded the note and replaced it with the locket in the box. She opened her wardrobe and placed the box in the drawer. It was hidden by her underwear. *This will be my secret,* she resolved silently. Knowing how Bella would react to something so significant from her past, she made a promise to herself: *Nobody will know about it, not even Bella.*

The first few weeks at Half Way House were hectic. Bella was eager to find a job and Annie talked regularly with Mrs Constable about her hopes and dreams. When Bella confronted her about it, she was taken aback. "Why are you sucking up to Constable?" she asked. "It doesn't look good, Annie. How many times do I have to tell you? Be your own boss and stand on your own two feet.

Three

A month later, Annie and Bella had secured jobs. Bella was working as a waitress in the Pike House Hotel and came home every week with a basic wage that was increased by tips given to her by satisfied guests.

Annie, on the other hand, had taken Sister Agatha's advice and had decided to study at Bolton Technical College to complete her advanced level exams in maths, biology and chemistry. She worked in Woolworths until September when college resumed after the summer holidays. Once college resumed, she would work as a Saturday girl and would be able to do extra shifts during the holidays.

When she announced her intensions to Bella, she was greeted as usual with Bella's mocking opinion. "You must be joking, Annie," she said. "Why would you want to go to college? That's for mugs who think the grass is greener on the other side."

Annie was determined not to be browbeaten anymore by Bella and she gathered all her courage to say firmly, "Are you happy with your job as a waitress, Bella?"

"'Course I am. What do you mean by that little Miss Smarty Pants?" Bella's hackles were rising. "How come you're so high and mighty all of a sudden? Has that snooty Doreen Blackburn got in your ear? She and that lad—what's his name—John Lawton, were studying in the drawing room when we arrived."

"Just listen for a minute, will you, Bella? Nobody has got in my ear, as you put it, and if you are enjoying working at the restaurant, I'm pleased for you, but don't tell me I'm doing the wrong thing, because I know I'm doing what's right for me."

"*I've* always known what's right for you, Annie. I've always had your back. I'm older than you and I can stand up to people when you are too weak and scared to speak up," Bella said with more than a little venom in her tone.

Annie sighed. "I'm not disputing that, Bella, and I'm grateful you have been my forever friend, but I've grown up now and I'm able to stand on my own two feet. Please give me that at least."

Bella looked completely crushed. "So you don't need me anymore? I see. Well, you can sod off, Annie. I have Jack at work now and he's asked me out on a date, so I can manage without your friendship. See if I care."

Annie, in turn, looked crushed too. "I didn't say that, Bella. All I wanted was for you to be happy for me, but it seems you can't even do that. I appreciate that you have always been there for me and I don't think I would have survived St Anthony's without you, but please don't turn against me just because I'm not doing what you are doing. We are different..."

"Different? Oh that's it, is it? We swore to be blood sisters a few years ago. Does all that count for nothing? I just don't understand you anymore, Annie. All that studying has gone to your head," Bella told her and walked towards the door.

Both girls were flushed and there was awkwardness between them for the first time in their young lives. "I'm here if you need me," Annie called gently.

Bella stopped in her tracks. "If *I* need *you?*" she retorted and walked off before Annie could respond.

~ * ~

During the following few weeks, Bella kept her distance from Annie. After dinner every night, each went to her own room. They passed the time of day with each other, but the atmosphere was chilly until Bella, wearing a new dress and frilly underskirt, appeared in the drawing room one night where Annie was studying. "I treated myself from my tips," she told Annie as though the argument never happened. "These net underskirts are all the rage. You should get one, Annie, if you can afford it. I've bought some trews too. Black Watch tartan and a thick sloppy joe sweater. I love having money to spend."

"I noticed the trews earlier. They are lovely," Annie said, "And your dress looks very pretty, especially with those white shoes. You look really nice, Bella, and when did you get your hair done like that?"

Bella preened. "This afternoon at Gladys Little's in Farnworth. One of the guests at the hotel told me about her salon. Does it suit me?"

Annie waved her hand to indicate that Bella should turn around. Bella twirled to show off her new styling to her advantage and Annie told her again that she looked lovely.

"Are you going out tonight?" she asked.

"I'm going out with Jack," Bella replied. "I've been going out with him for six weeks now. I never knew how boys could make you feel..."

"How do you mean?" Annie asked.

Bella smiled and Annie gasped at how lovely she looked, her flicked black hair bobbing attractively as she danced around and her new pink gingham dress with frilly underskirt made her look stunningly beautiful. "You should get a boyfriend, then you'd know," Bella suggested and she winked knowingly.

Annie, determined not to be made to look naïve, smiled her most genuine smile and said, "I haven't time for a boyfriend just yet. I know a few boys at college, but I want to be a nurse and that means I must pass my A levels so I can do the link course to nursing." She paused and then said, "I'm glad we are friends again though."

"Oh Annie, Annie, Annie," Bella wailed with more than a little sarcasm in her tone. "You don't know what you're missing. I'll introduce you to one of Jack's mates if you like."

"Thanks, but no thanks, Bella," Annie cut in. "You enjoy yourself. I'm fine as I am."

"Okay, Annie O'Shea, but I'll keep trying, you know. I'll get you to have a bit of fun instead of poring over those books day in and day out. Nobody rules our lives now, or haven't you noticed?" Bella slowly shook her head in mock disbelief and then tripped merrily out of the door to meet her date.

Four

Bella's renaissance

The restaurant manager at Pike House Hotel was impressed with Bella's confidence and the way she picked up silver service. "If you carry on like this," he told her, "you'll soon be ready for private functions too."

"I told you at my interview I was a quick learner," she replied as she felt a rush of self-satisfaction course through her veins.

"Just one thing though, Bella," the manager continued. "Try not to be too familiar with our guests.

"I am just being friendly, Mr Winters."

"I know that, but asking them where they live and what their jobs are is really none of your business, is it?" Winters said.

Bella felt her face redden, something she hadn't experienced before. "I just wondered how far they'd travelled to come to this restaurant. It's really miles from everywhere round here and it's not cheap either."

"Just don't ask, Bella. We don't want to lose our clientele," Winters concluded.

Bella shrugged. "Okay, Mr Winters. Message received loud and clear."

Harry Winters shook his head slowly as he walked away. *She's a headstrong girl, that one, but she's the best waitress we've ever had. Let's hope she heeds what I told her.*

~ * ~

Jack Spencer was the bar manager and noticed Bella as soon as she hit the dining room like a whirlwind. "Crikey Moses, young 'un, which express train did you arrive on?"

Bella glared at him. "What do you mean?" she asked indignantly.

"I've never seen anybody move so quick round them tables," Jack remarked. "Where have you come from? I haven't seen you around here before."

"That's for me to know and for you to find out," she quipped.

"Oh, and she's quick-witted too," Jack said as he winked to the other barman, Rick. "I think I'll have to take you in hand, young lady." And he winked at Rick again who laughed at Jack's suggestive remark.

"You'll have to catch me first, mister," came the fast reply and Bella disappeared into the pantry to collect the cutlery for her station before opening time.

Bella worked shifts from six-thirty in the morning until five in the afternoon for the early shift and from four-thirty until midnight on the late shift. "They are funny times, Mrs Constable, but I don't mind."

Mrs Constable looked pensive. "How do you get there so early in the morning, Bella, and how do you get back so late at night?

"The hotel bus picks me up and drops me off whichever time it is," she told Mrs Constable. "But you needn't worry about me 'cos I can get a lift off Jack Spencer. He has a car and I know he'll give me a lift if I ask him."

"Who is Jack Spencer?" Mrs Constable asked.

"He's the bar manager at Pike House."

"And how do you know he'll give you a lift?" the motherly woman asked.

Bella grinned. "He likes me."

Mrs Constable raised her eyebrows and asked, "How much does he like you?"

Bella was irritated. "Why do you ask that?" she snapped. "It doesn't matter how much. I don't wish to be rude, but it really isn't any of your business, is it?"

"Oh Bella." Mrs Constable sighed and put her hand on Bella's shoulder. "You have recently come from an all girls' institution. Men and boys are alien to you. Just be careful, please. That's all I'll say at the moment."

~ * ~

It was a few days after Mrs Constable's motherly warning that Jack asked Bella if he might take her out on her day off. "How would you like to go to Blackpool on Friday? I've checked with Mr Winters and he says it's your day off on the same day as mine."

"What's at Blackpool?" Bella asked innocently.

"You mean you've never been to Blackpool?" Jack asked in amazement.

"I've never been anywhere. If you'd been brought up in St Anthony's, you wouldn't have been anywhere either," Bella informed him.

"Aw you poor little thing," he said mockingly.

"Don't joke about that, Jack. It was no picnic and I'm only just getting used to being able to please myself what I do and don't do. Be careful, or I'll say no to your invitation if you start making fun of my situation."

"Sorry," Jack said genuinely, "but will you go out with me?"

Bella thought for a moment. "Okay," she replied with a resigned tone in her voice. "What do I wear on a date in Blackpool?"

"Trews and a sweater. It gets a bit chilly on Blackpool prom," Jack told her. "You can put a jacket in the car in case you need it."

"I'll be at the end of Greenhough Lane at ten o'clock. Don't be late."

At nine-thirty on that particular Friday, Bella was ready to leave. The night before, she'd had a run-in with Annie so she was glad to be going out all day so as not to have to see her. She signed out of Half Way House as required and ran happily down the drive to the end of Greenhough Lane. She wore her new trews and a pale blue tee-shirt with a pretty scalloped edging at the V-neck and round the edge of the cap sleeves and hem. She carried her thick sloppy joe thrown over her shoulder bag. The sun was shining and the forecast said it was going to be a hot day.

She arrived at the end of the lane early. Jack wasn't there. She smiled to herself. *I'm glad he's not here. I don't want him to see me coming out of Half Way House. He knows I live there, but ... well, I don't want him to see me there. As soon as I can, I'll get a place of my own. Now won't that be fantastic?*

Jack pulled up in his pale yellow Ford Anglia. "Hello, Bella Jones. What are you doing standing on the street corner at this time of day?" he joked.

"I'm waiting for somebody," she answered, "if he ever turns up."

"Will I do instead of who you're waiting for?" Jack asked, continuing the amusing little scenario.

"I suppose so if you're all that's on offer," she said resignedly.

"Come on, get in the car before the sun stops shining," Jack coaxed. "I'd like to get to Blackpool sometime today." He leaned over to open the door and Bella got in.

Before they set off, Jack enquired, "If it's not a rude question, how old are you, Bella?"

"Why do you need to know?" she asked indignantly.

"I'm curious, that's all. I'm twenty-three and I don't want to be accused of cradle-snatching," he said with caution.

"I'm not a baby," she answered, not hiding her irritation.

"I know that, but you look young so I'm hoping you might be over sixteen," he went on.

She looked squarely at him and pressed her lips tightly together as if to be preparing to impart bad news. Jack's anxious expression made her smile. "Relax, old man," she said cheekily. "I'm eighteen, nineteen in August...I think."

Then it was Jack's turn to smile. "You think?" he teased.

"How would I know?" she said, more seriously now. "I don't have a birth certificate so the nuns assigned the date they found me on the doorstep."

"How sad," Jack sympathised.

"It's just the way it is," she said matter-of-factly. "I got the nineteenth of August, nineteen forty, so there you have it. Now, let's get going."

They drove along the A6 through Chorley, then Preston before they saw Blackpool Tower in the distance. "Look at that!" Jack said excitedly. "Your first glimpse of Blackpool Tower!"

"Where?" Bella asked. "What am I looking for?"

Jack pulled over to the side of the road and pointed out the tall spike-like structure in the distance.

Bella was unimpressed. "What's it for?" she asked. "It just looks like a big toothpick to me. What does it do?"

Jack grinned. "It doesn't do anything as such," he explained. "It was built in the style of the Eiffel Tower in Paris. You can go up to the top of it in a lift and there is a ballroom with a Wurlitzer organ and a zoo in the buildings underneath. There's a cafeteria too and an aquarium and the Tower Circus is famous all over the world."

"Blimey!" Bella exclaimed. "I've never heard of it. The nuns never talked much about what was outside the convent. I wish I'd known about Blackpool Tower then. I'd have run away to Blackpool never to be seen again."

"Get away with you," Jack said. "The police would have found you and dragged you back kicking and screaming."

"I would not kick and scream, Jack Spencer. I would have just gone back and done it again the following week," she told him, displaying the ever defiant trait in her character.

"I bet you would too," he agreed. "Feisty little devil, aren't you? But I like that." His thoughts were more sympathetic than judgemental. *There's something about her that's captivating and yet she's very naïve about many things. I'd like to think there's someone who needs to be loved under that hard exterior.*

They arrived at South Shore and parked the car near to the Pleasure Beach. Bella was awestruck. "What on earth is that?" she asked as she saw the carriages on the big dipper fly around the track and heard the excited screams of those who were in the carriages.

"We'll go on that later," Jack promised. "First we'll go on a tram along the prom and get off at the North Pier.

They crossed the road to the tram stop and Bella gasped again. "Look, Jack, look!" she shrieked like an excited child. "The sea! I've never seen the sea before. Oh thanks for bringing me here. If I die now, I'll die happy because you have opened up a whole new world to me." Tears glistened in her eyes and Jack saw the vulnerable child usually hidden by the brick wall she built around herself.

"Don't cry," he said gently.

Bella brushed away the tears that trickled down her cheeks and pulled herself up abruptly. "I'm not crying," she said. "I never cry. Not even when Sister Josephine slapped my legs for not learning my times tables. It's the wind coming off the sea that's making my eyes water."

Jack felt every part of his body tense with pity for this girl, but he chose not to comment on her past. "Okay," he said. He offered her his handkerchief to dry her tears. "Look, here's the tram."

The green and cream tram trundled to the stopping point. "This is brilliant!" Bella stated with more confidence than she had shown a few minutes earlier. "It's like a bus running on train lines."

They climbed on the tram and Jack paid the conductor once they were in their seats. Bella sat by the window so she wouldn't miss any of the sights. Jack pointed out South Pier as they passed. "Can we walk to the end of the pier after, Jack? We will be walking over the sea and I can see people fishing off the end."

"Okay," Jack told her. "We'll get off the tram at North Pier and walk along that one if you like."

"Are there two piers then?"

"There are three actually: South, Central and North," Jack explained.

Bella gazed in awe at everything as Jack pointed out first the donkeys on the beach carrying children along the shore. Some of the children were laughing and others seemed nervously serious as they sat on the donkeys' backs. Others looked very proud, sitting bolt upright but clinging to the reins as if their lives were in danger.

They passed Central Pier and the Tower and soon arrived at North Pier where Jack told her they would get off the tram. He jumped down first and then turned to offer Bella his hand. Ignoring his help, she jumped down herself. Jack shook his head. "All right, Miss Independent, point taken."

From Bella's point of view, the day kept getting better and better. She learned how to play on the slot machines and grew increasingly annoyed when she kept losing the pennies she'd won.

"Nobody ever wins on those things," Jack told her.

"I did! I won a shilling and then lost it again!" Bella said haughtily.

"That's what they want you to do," Jack explained.

"Who?" she asked.

"Whoever owns the machines," Jack said. "Come on, let's leave before we're bankrupt!"

"I don't understand that," she told him.

"Neither do I really, but let's go in the Tower cafeteria and have something to eat. We'll have a quick look round the Tower afterwards and then we'll stroll down the prom to the Pleasure Beach."

As they strolled along the sea front, Jack took her hand in his. Bella thrilled at his touch. She looked shyly at him and he smiled at her. Her thoughts were confused. *Oh my Lord. What is happening to me? Why have I got butterflies in my stomach just because he's holding my hand? This is nothing like Sister Agatha said it would be if a boy touched me. She said I would feel sick and must not allow skin to touch skin at any time. Well, Sister Agatha...his hand touching mine feels wonderful, so all you said in those 'Lessons on Life' was a load of rubbish. I like...*

"A penny for them," Jack offered.

"A penny for what?"

"Your thoughts, silly. I can see I'm going to have to teach you all about life in the big wide world," Jack informed her jokingly.

Bella nudged him gently. "I'm a quick learner, and for your information, my thoughts would be worth much more than a penny, Jack Spencer."

"Would they now?" he replied with a smile. "I see. Here we are then. I'm sure you'll love the Pleasure Beach."

The Pleasure Beach was indeed everything she could never have imagined. There were all sorts of rides, each giving a thrill better than the previous one. They went on the Ferris wheel first and then the Waltzer. Both rides made her insides retch with excitement, but that was nothing to how she felt on the Big Dipper and the Grand National. "I don't think I should have had fish and chips in the cafe," she announced. "I almost brought them back on the Grand National. But it's a good way of nearly throwing up!"

"We'll go on a more gentle ride now then," Jack told her and he led her to a ride called the Caterpillar. It was a series of carriages running along a track that went up and down as it sped round. She and Jack sat side by side and the centrifugal force threw them together so that their bodies were stuck tight. They were unable to fight the force so Jack put his arm around her and turned her head towards him. Suddenly, a canopy came up and over the carriages and all went dark. Jack's lips found Bella's and he kissed her lovingly. In spite of her inexperience, her lips opened to allow his probing tongue to play with her sensibilities.

Oh Jesus, Mary and Joseph, she thought. *I should push him away...I should push him away...I should...Oh my...* and the canopy opened up to reveal blushing young ladies and proud young men in each carriage busily straightening clothes and sitting bolt upright as though nothing had happened.

Bella was dumbstruck and Jack gave her a confident hug. "I think we'd better be making our way back. It'll be getting late by the time we're back in Bolton."

Bella nodded, but remained pensively quiet on the way home. Jack left her alone with her thoughts and the silence between them was poignant, but not uncomfortable.

~ * ~

During the next few weeks, Bella and Jack worked together at Pike House Hotel and spent their days off together too. Sometimes they went to the Odeon or the Lido in town and saw a film. Bella loved the films as she had never been to a cinema before meeting Jack. The nearest she had come to watching a film was when the nuns used a cinematograph to explain a scientific theory or to show what life was like in the Holy Land, but that wasn't very often.

During July 1959, Bella relied on Jack's friendship more than she had relied on anybody previously. Her row with Annie had made her realise that as they grew older, they would grow apart when they wanted different things for the future. Bella had met Jack at a very convenient time for her. He became an important part of her life and she also appreciated the girls she worked with because they knew what life was all about. She went shopping in Bolton each week and her wardrobe was becoming full of fashionable clothes and pretty accessories. The day she bought her pink and white gingham dress and frilly underskirt, she had wanted to show Annie more than anyone.

Bella knew by heart everything she had said when they had their disagreement. She remembered the aggressive nature of her words and the sorrow she felt as she walked away from Annie. Suddenly, she appeared in front of Annie again as though the row never happened. She knew Annie was taken by surprise, but happy that the situation seemed to have resolved itself with her new wardrobe. Annie told her she looked lovely. "And you look very happy too," she added. "Are you going out tonight?"

"I'm going out with Jack," Bella replied. "I've been with him for six weeks now."

"I'm pleased for you, Bella and I must say I have never seen you look so ... so radiant. Perhaps having a boyfriend is good for you." She wanted to say, *I told you something wonderful would happen,* but she kept her thoughts to herself.

~ * ~

Jack took Bella to the Bodega Club in Manchester that night. "The band plays traditional jazz and I think you'll like it," he told her as they drove along Market Street in Farnworth on the way to Manchester.

"What's this town called?" Bella asked. "There are a lot of people around and they're all dressed up. There must be some good places here to go for a good night out."

"It's Farnworth," he told her.

"Oh, I came here to get my hair done, but not round here," she said, looking around to get her bearings. "The hairdressers was in an arcade place where the buses stop."

'Oh, that's just over there on King Street," Jack informed her. "There are a lot of good pubs here, but I think lots of people go to the Monaco. They have dancing and sometimes live groups. I remember Adam Faith appearing there," Jack told her. "I'll take you there sometime if you like."

"I don't know how to dance, Jack. I'd feel stupid."

"I'll teach you then," Jack assured her.

"How much farther to Manchester? It seems a long way away." Bella was fidgeting and her net underskirt was scratching her nylons with sitting in the car. "My stockings are going to be in shreds before we get there and then what will I look like?"

"You'll be fine, Bella. Stop whinging. We'll be there in about half an hour."

"Half an hour? Blimey!" But she chose not to complain anymore. *Jack looks a bit annoyed,* she thought. *Don't rock the boat, Bella. I like him and he's been good to me. Now I've made my peace with Annie, she would tell me to show some appreciation, so...*

The music in the Bodega Club got their feet tapping and some couples were jiving on the tiny dance floor in front of the Manchester University Jazz Band playing that night. Bella watched with great interest, but when Jack asked if she wanted to give it a try, she shook her head vigorously. "I'll learn first and then I might dance, but not yet."

She sampled her first alcoholic drink: brandy and Babycham. It was like nothing she had ever tasted and the bubbles tickled her nose, but when she'd had a couple, she began to feel happy with everything, with Jack in particular. He noticed and squeezed her hand in appreciation.

It was gone eleven o'clock when they left the jazz club and Bella rested her head on Jack's shoulder as he drove home. They drove via

Scout Road and over the moors out of Bolton towards Belmont and Jack pulled over to the side of the road.

"Are we home?" Bella asked sleepily.

"Not yet, but let's just get in the back of the car for a kiss and a cuddle," Jack invited.

Bella did as she was asked and snuggled up close to Jack once he had closed the door.

Their kisses were soft and gentle and Bella sighed with delight. Her arms were round his neck and he pulled her close so he could feel the beat of her heart and the softness of her breasts on his chest. His kisses became more urgent and he groaned as he kissed her waiting lips. "Oh Bella," he groaned. "I love you so much."

"Oh my..." Bella was in heaven and Jack had declared his love for her. Her head was spinning and she kissed him more ardently, her tongue and his teasing and flicking as they pushed their emotions to way beyond anything in her experience. Their breathing was thick and heavy. Jack's hands caressed her body, lingering on her breasts as she groaned in sheer delight. His right hand found her legs and he inched up towards her stocking tops. Bella's thoughts were wild. *Never allow skin on skin, Sister Agatha had said, but I can't stop, Sister... I have to go to wherever Jack is taking me. Get thee behind me, Sister bloomin' Agatha.* Jack was on top of her and...

Afterwards, she wept. Jack held her close to comfort her. "Bella," he said falteringly. "I would never do anything to hurt you. Please believe me."

"I don't know what to say," Bella answered as she dried her tears. "Sister Agatha...well, she didn't tell us *that* happens when you fall in love."

"In the real world, *that* actually does happen, sweetheart," Jack told her seriously. "Some guys go out with girls just for *that* and then when they've got what they want, they move on to the next girl who's willing."

Bella looked horrified. "Are you finding another girl now?" she asked, tears rising in her eyes again.

"Of course not," he reassured. "I said I love you and I meant it. Making love to you was so natural."

"Will we do it every time we go out?" she asked. Her innocence and naïvete were endearing.

Jack laughed. "Oh Bella!" he said as he pecked her on the cheek. "I love you, but we'll do it when we both want to."

"What if I want to every time I see you?"

Jack was taken aback. "Well then, we'll see how it goes."

He drove her back to Half Way House. It was a long way past midnight and Mrs Constable would be waiting for her to return. Fortunately Bella had signed out and had told Annie where she was going. She had a key, but she knew Mrs Constable would still wait up until she returned. She went in as quietly as she could and carefully closed the door behind her.

Out of the shadows, Mrs Constable appeared in her dressing gown and slippers. "My goodness, Bella! You look a mess! What have you been up to?"

Five

Annie's emergence

Annie settled into Half Way House much quicker than she thought she would. She made friends with the other guests and realised that those friendships didn't last long, because once those people found permanent jobs, or qualified to go into teacher training college or university, they left Half Way House to find their own way in the world independently. It made her realise, too, that Bella was more than a friend to her, but the day she stood up for herself and dared to contradict Bella, she wondered if she should have just said nothing to keep the peace and not harm their friendship.

She was unable to forget everything Bella had said to her in those moments of anger.

She said she thought I was joking. Why would I want to go to college? She thought college for mugs who think the grass is greener on the other side. Why couldn't she just be happy for me? Why would she think I had allowed somebody else to influence my decision? When I told her I had made the decision by myself, she questioned my ability to do such a thing and expected me to let her decide what my future should be. I hope we can get over our differences, but the way Bella is at the moment, I think she might just forget about us as we were and carry on with her life without me. That would be sad and it would break my heart.

At work one Saturday, Annie saw Bella pass Woolworth's front entrance on Deansgate. She was arm in arm with a girl Annie didn't recognise, talking and laughing without a care in the world. Annie's heart skipped a beat. *Maybe she doesn't need me anymore.*

With that thought in her head, Annie brushed away a tear that had somehow found its way to trickle down her cheek. She took a deep breath and continued to stack the shelves under the counter with products that ran out almost as soon as they appeared in the store. Her feet ached and she still had two more hours until closing time.

"Take your break now, Annie," called the supervisor.

"Thanks, Margot. I'm ready for it."

"Are you okay, love?" Margot asked. "You look a bit peaky."

Annie managed a smile. "I'm all right. Just a bit tired today. It seems to have been a long one."

"I know what you mean, love. Go and have a cuppa and then it will be nearly closing time. Are you out tonight?" Margot liked to show interest in her girls.

"No, I'm not. I have an essay to finish. Holiday assignment," Annie explained.

Margot pursed her lips. "Ecky thump, Annie love, you're far too pretty to be studying on a Saturday night. You look like a miniature version of Petula Clark. Small, but perfectly formed. That's you, of course. Petula Clark is all right, but I think you have the edge on her. I bet there are plenty of lads who'd like a date with you."

Annie screwed up her nose. "You sound like my friend. She keeps on about finding me a boyfriend, but I don't know. I've only met a few boys at college and in Half Way House, but none who I'd go on a date with. I wouldn't know what to say to them."

Margot burst out laughing. "Yer don't have to say anythin' if yer don't want to." She laughed out loud again. "God bless yer little cotton socks, Annie. The boys'll know what to say and what to do on a date. You'd just have to go with the flow. Go and have yer brew. It'll make yer feel better."

On the bus on the way home, Annie thought about what Margot had said. *You're far too pretty not to have a boyfriend,* or words to that effect. She also thought about how happy Bella appeared since she had been going out with Jack. *But I'm content as I am. I'm going to pass my A levels and apply to nursing college. That will be the first thing on my wish list and I can think about meeting boys after that.*

The journey home from work gave Annie time to reflect on what had happened earlier with Bella. She had appeared in a new dress and she had had her hair done in a new style. Annie noted that she looked lovely, but as Bella hadn't really spoken to her since their falling out, she decided not to say anything. However, she did smile at her lifelong friend who had more recently felt like a stranger to her. On reflection, it was the turning point in their relationship. Annie closed her eyes as she looked back on the situation. She had been surprised when Bella walked over to speak to her as if the argument had never happened. The bus rattled along and Annie made herself more comfortable in her seat. *I think she thought I'd be envious of all her new clothes, but I don't think I could ever be jealous of Bella. It would be like begrudging everything she has achieved. She told me I should get a boyfriend because of the way it made her feel. I didn't understand that at all, but even Margot said I should get a boyfriend so there must be something in it.*

Annie smiled to herself as she connected Bella's comments to what Margot had said to her that afternoon. *I was so determined not to be made to look naïve, so I smiled my most genuine smile and told her I hadn't got time for a boyfriend just yet.* The conductor called out, "Next stop Greenhough Lane," and Annie was jolted from her reverie.

As she walked down the driveway to Half Way House, she wondered why she would remember, word for word, the reconnection with Bella. *See yer later, alligator, she said.*

Annie laughed at the memory. Her thoughts even now were self-critical. *I have some nice clothes too and I will get to wear them sometime, but Bella is, in spite of everything, so different from me. Face it, girl, peas in a pod you are not! At one point we seemed to be joined at the hip, but the separation has been coming for a while. Still, we can be friends without living in each other's pockets, at least I hope we can.*

That Saturday night, Annie stayed in the drawing room to finish her essay, but the new television set was on and she couldn't concentrate. She looked around at the guests, who, like herself, were spending Saturday in. She noticed that the younger girls all sat huddled together on the sofa and the boys, only three of them, sat on the floor in a little group, completely ignoring the girls. As Annie observed them, one of the boys caught her eye and he boldly winked at her. Wide eyed, she covered her mouth with her hand so he wouldn't see her grinning in amusement. Slowly, the young man got up from the floor and wandered over to her.

"Well, Annie O'Shea, why aren't you out on the town on a Saturday night?" he asked, his arms folded as though he were ready to interrogate her.

Taken aback by his friendly manner, Annie put down her pen and leaned forward, placing her elbows on the table. "Well, since you ask, David Anderson, I'm trying to finish an assignment on the circulation of the blood and the effects of anaemia on the functions of the body."

"Oh," he said. "I thought an essay on comparing and contrasting Hamlet's relationships with his mother and with Ophelia was bad enough, but trying to write about anything anatomical or scientific would fill me with dread."

Annie was impressed. "Well, I guess trying to do anything in here is virtually impossible with Hughie Green telling the contestants that he means everything *'most sincerely, folks,'* not to mention Dixon of Dock Green's *'Evenin' all.'* I really ought to go back to my room."

"Oh don't do that," David said, his expression one of disappointment.

"Why not?" Annie asked. "I'll never finish my essay down here, will I?"

David shrugged, his shoulders seeming to swallow his neck momentarily and Annie saw for the first time that she was looking at a very attractive, tanned, dark haired young man whom she had seen before, but of whom she had never really taken much notice.

"Can I make you a coffee?" he asked.

"That would be nice," Annie said, "but I might have to take it back to my room. I meant it when I said I have to finish this assignment."

"Can't it wait until tomorrow? I've only just plucked up the courage to talk to you. Don't run away from me now. I'm not that scary, am I?" David's face was turning a rather delicate shade of rosy pink and Annie noticed.

"All right then," she declared, feeling his embarrassment so much that she felt her face changing colour too.

As they drank their coffee away from the other guests who were still glued to the television screen, conversation was surprisingly easy and friendly. David had voluntarily entered Half Way House to escape his drunken father. His mother had passed away when he was a baby and his grandparents died when he was fourteen, so he applied to the Angels' Charity to live in Half Way House until he finished his secondary education and he intended to go to university.

"I thought we were all orphans in this place," Annie told him. "It never entered my head that you could come in voluntarily."

"Well, now you know," he said. "Technically, I'm an abandoned child. My dad was and is incapable of looking after himself, let alone making sure I have everything I need. What about you?"

Annie thought for a moment before she answered. "I was left at St Anthony's when I was two years old. It was pretty grim, but the nuns did their best...well, most of them. A few were driven by rules and the fear of God's wrath, but as long as we toed the line, we survived without too much hassle. Which school do you go to, David? Do they know about your situation?"

"I'm in the Sixth Form at the Anglican grammar school, and yes they do. They've known from the time when I appeared in school with bruises on my face and legs. They were very helpful in securing my place here at Half Way House. I know it's run by a Catholic charity, but fortunately, Mrs Constable is a strong supporter of religious unity and she put forward a good case for me with Social Services." David was comfortable talking to Annie and it showed. "I used to study with John Lawton. He was so committed to his studies and I admired his ambition. I wonder how he's getting on at university. He's studying to be a doctor. I don't think he ever knew his parents either, so he must be very proud of himself. I hope I can do as well as he has, but I don't want to be a doctor or anything like that."

"What do you want to do when you leave the grammar school?" Annie asked. "*I* want to be a nurse. Ever since I was a little girl, I didn't want to be anything else. I have no idea why. Maybe it's something in my genes. Who knows?"

David was impressed. "You'll make a good nurse, I'm sure," he told her. "I want to go into teaching. I'm doing A level English Literature, History and Art History. I really want to try to get into Oxford or Cambridge. Unfortunately, I think Oxbridge is very exclusive, so I don't think I have much chance of a place, but any red brick university would also be okay so long as I am able to move away from Bolton. I need to spread my wings a little."

"I hope your dreams come true," Annie said and she looked at the clock on the mantelpiece. "Goodness, it's eleven o'clock. I was expecting Bella to be back by now."

David's face was a picture of complete amusement. "I can't say I know Bella at all, but from what I've seen of her, I wouldn't think she bothers too much about rules and social niceties. I wish I could be as carefree as she seems to be, but I owe so much to this place and I'm going to make sure I do what is necessary to keep in Mrs C's good books."

"Me too," Annie agreed, "But don't worry about Bella. She is often a law unto herself, but she's loyal to her friends. That I can say with certainty. She does have a soft side under her hard exterior."

"Well, goodnight, Annie O'Shea. I hope we can do this again sometime." David touched her sleeve gently as they walked towards the stairs.

"I would like that," Annie told him. "Goodnight, David."

~ * ~

The following morning, Annie noticed that Bella wasn't at breakfast so as soon as she'd had her own, she went to Bella's room to find out what was happening. Cautiously, she knocked on the door of ME7 and waited. There was no reply. She knocked again, this time more forcefully. "Bella, it's me, Annie. Can I come in?"

There was a shuffling of feet behind the closed door and a tear-stained face appeared as the door opened slowly.

"Bella! What on earth is the matter?"

"Come in," Bella murmured. "I've had a terrible night. Mrs Constable read me the riot act when I got in last night. She said I'd been up to no good and I should be ashamed of myself, and Annie, I hadn't done anything wrong. What I did was so enjoyable...wonderful... honest...the stuff your dreams are made of."

"Hold on a minute, Bella," Annie interrupted. "Are you saying you've been thinking about my dreams, those dreams you told me were for mugs? But what's all this? I have never, and I mean never, seen you cry."

Bella sniffed and a sort of resigned impish grin spread across her face. She related only what Mrs Constable had said when she returned... *'Look at you, Bella; lipstick smudged across your face; your stockings laddered; your hair looking like you have just got out of bed...'* Mrs Constable assumed the worst and said I was disgraceful and if my behaviour doesn't improve, I'll have to leave Half Way House before my time here is completed. I only have another six months here anyway. That's what we were told, weren't we? Two years, providing we have mapped out a secure future."

Annie frowned. "Well, yes, but I don't really understand, Bella. What had you been doing? I thought you were going to a jazz club in Manchester."

"I did," Bella assured her, "but Jack and I had been kissing and cuddling in the car..."

Annie grinned. "So that's what you meant when you said I needed a boyfriend to find out how it made you feel. So what's Mrs C's problem? Surely she's been young herself."

Bella took a deep breath. "She just assumed the worst about me, Annie." She looked at the floor while she recovered her composure. "She can think what she likes, but I'm going to look for a flat as soon as possible."

"Wow, Bella! That's drastic, isn't it, just because of a bit of smudged lipstick?" Annie remarked with astonishment.

"Well, I don't want to feel like she's watching my every move, Annie," Bella said. "We've had enough of that in our previous lives and I'll be twenty soon so it's about time I started thinking about my future."

Annie stared at her, wide-eyed. "I can't believe how much you have changed. At one time, you behaved as though the whole world was against you. Be careful, Bella Jones. You'll be dreaming next!"

Bella gave her friend a playful nudge. "I don't think so, Annie, but I like where I'm at just now." *That's as much as Annie needs to know for the time being. I'm sure she wouldn't understand making love. I didn't either until it happened. My night of passion with Jack is for me to know and for nobody else to find out and that includes nosey Mrs Constable.*

Six

Following her run-in with Mrs Constable, Bella was careful not to arrive home late and she refrained from wearing lipstick when she went out with Jack. She and Annie spent more time together, mainly at mealtimes and occasionally before Bella went on her late shift. "Guess what I'm doing on my day off?" she challenged Annie one morning at breakfast several weeks later.

"Goodness, Bella, it could be anything, knowing you," Annie replied. "I hope it's not eloping to Gretna Green!"

"Don't be daft, Annie," Bella chided. "You know what I told you a few weeks ago about looking for somewhere else to live?"

Annie looked crest-fallen.

"Aw, Annie, don't look at me like that," she implored. "We both know we'll have to go our separate ways sometime. I'm twenty in August. I can't stay here forever."

"You are only nineteen now though and I know our two years are almost up, but I didn't think it would happen so soon. I still have to do my exams before I move on to the nursing course. I'll miss you."

"I'll have to look locally so as to be near work. Since I've been promoted to supervisor, my wage has increased and although you'd never believe it, I've been saving up for my deposit."

"My goodness," Annie declared, looking out of the window. "There must be pigs flying out there somewhere. Well done, you! I'm proud of you. Would you like me to go looking at flats with you?"

Bella pressed her lips together and blushed. "No, thanks, Annie. Jack says he'll help me find the right place. He's just turned twenty-five and he's still living at home with his parents so I'm not sure he knows what to look for, but I said he could help."

"Have you met his parents?" Annie asked.

Bella shrugged. "Not yet."

"Isn't that a bit strange, considering you've been going out with him for well over a year now?" Annie saw Bella's expression change from glowing with enthusiasm to confused uncertainty.

"I have never asked him why he doesn't take me to meet them. It's really no big deal for me since I can't take him to meet my parents, can I? I guess he doesn't want me to feel awkward. I don't even know his address. I never asked, but I know he doesn't live far from work so he must be somewhere in Rivington or Horwich or maybe Belmont. He could live anywhere, couldn't he?"

Annie grinned. "He must live somewhere, Bella, or he could have a mattress behind the bar that you can't see!"

They both laughed. "Look at us, Annie! We're laughing! Who'd have thought a couple of years ago that we could laugh like this?"

"I know," Annie agreed. "It makes me feel so good to be alive! Maybe we were dead and have come back to life again."

"That's what it feels like," Bella agreed. "If only we'd known what life outside was like. It was only something to wonder about, wasn't it?"

"Or dream about," Annie put in.

Bella gave Annie a playful nudge. "I wouldn't go that far, Annie O'Shea. You know what I think about dreamers. I feel better now I've unloaded all my worries onto you. Thanks. I owe you one. Well, I'd better be off, or Mr Winters will take my promotion off me."

~ * ~

Annie's studies took priority over anything else. She still worked on Saturdays and put her money in the bank with most of the fifty pounds Sister Agatha had given her when she left St Anthony's. She'd bought a few clothes when she had been able to work more than one day a week and she prided herself on her appearance, even though her life didn't offer much socialising. After the exams in June, she would be on holiday until college started so she would be working more and increasing her bank balance. She usually studied with David and a couple of times they had been to the Central Library in Bolton because it was quiet.

It was on the bus one afternoon travelling back from the library that David shocked Annie. She was looking out of the window as she usually did. She saw something different every time she passed the countryside north of Bolton and she was absorbed with the view of yachts on Belmont reservoir. Suddenly, David took hold of her hand and, mortified, she snatched it away. "What are you doing?" she asked in her panic.

David blushed profusely. "Sorry," he said, "I didn't think you'd mind."

"Well, I do," Annie said feeling her cheeks burning.

David sighed and then breathed in deeply to regain his composure. "Annie, I like you and I thought you liked me. People who like each other hold hands when they are together. It seems I've got it all wrong." He sighed again and folded his arms so as not to further offend her.

Annie felt tears rising in her eyes and turned to look out of the window again. She blinked hard to send the tears back from where they came, but her efforts were all in vain. The tears trickled down her cheeks and she tried to wipe them away discreetly. Seeing her plight, David offered her his handkerchief and whispered, "I'm sorry."

They spent the rest of the journey in silence. They got off the bus at the end of Greenhough Lane and walked slowly towards Half Way House. David stuck his hands in his pockets and left enough space between himself and Annie in order not to give her cause to panic again. It was Annie who broke the silence as they approached the door of Half Way House.

"Can we just stop here for a minute?" she asked timidly.

David nodded and went to sit on the bench which faced the garden. Annie joined him. Boldly taking his hand in hers, she began, "I am so sorry I offended you."

David was surprised at her actions, but said, "No need to be sorry, Annie."

"Shush please, I need to say this. At St Anthony's, we were always told never to allow skin on skin when we were with boys." She deliberately patted his hand to emphasise her point.

David stifled a laugh.

"Don't laugh, David. I'm serious and I need to explain my earlier reaction to you," she stated firmly. "The nuns were adamant that if we let a boy touch us, we would certainly live to regret it. Information like that was imprinted in our brains. When you took my hand on the bus, I instinctively panicked, but it all seems pathetic now I've thought about it. I do like you, but I didn't think of you as a boyfriend, you know, a proper boyfriend."

"That's a pity," David interjected.

"Let me finish," Annie said. "You are the first real friend I've had who's a boy. Surely you noticed how awkward I was when you first came to speak to me."

David shrugged.

"Well, if you didn't notice, it *was* how I felt. I soon realised you weren't the devil incarnate, which was the way I had been taught to perceive the opposite sex."

"Annie," David interrupted, "I'm eighteen like you and I have never had a proper girlfriend. I have friends at school who are girls, but I don't fancy them at all. I have fancied you ever since you arrived at Half Way House and I only plucked up the courage to talk to you when I saw you without Bella that Saturday night a few weeks ago. Once we got talking, it confirmed I had been right to like you. I've been saving my allowance so that I might ask you out, but now I'm not so sure. I don't want to be humiliated when you refuse."

Annie was still holding his hands in hers. She squeezed gently. "Ask me," she encouraged.

David pulled his hands away from hers and Annie looked at him with disappointment etched all over her face. "Annie O'Shea..." He paused while he took a deep breath. "Would you like to go to the pictures with me on Saturday?"

Annie waited a few seconds and then said enthusiastically, "I would! What will we see? I've never been to a cinema. Bella told me how big the screens are and everything is in colour."

"You've never been to the cinema?" David was aghast.

"We were never allowed out on our own and the only films we saw at St Anthony's were religious or scientific," Annie explained.

David couldn't help smiling. "You are so unique, Annie," and then more boldly, "Please can I give you a hug?"

"That's not skin on skin, is it?" she queried with a smile. She moved closer to him and they hugged affectionately.

"There," David said. "That wasn't too bad, was it? Now what shall we see on Saturday? You choose. *GI Blues* with Elvis Presley or a western, *The Magnificent Seven?*"

"The girls in Woolworths were talking about Elvis Presley," Annie divulged. "They are all in love with him so they say. I think I might like to see who they were talking about so I can join in next time he crops up in the conversation. I just kept quiet last time. I didn't want to look stupid saying I didn't know who he was. They don't know I was brought up in an orphanage and I'd prefer to keep it that way."

"*GI Blues* it is then," David decided. "What time do you finish work on Saturday?"

"I don't finish until half past five," she said. "It's usually quarter past six when I get back here."

"I could meet you from work," David suggested. "We can go to Aristotle's for something to eat and then catch the first house at seven o'clock."

"That sounds lovely, but what's Aristotle's?" Annie asked.

"It's a Greek restaurant, but if you are unsure of Greek food, you can have English food in there as well as Greek," David assured her. "I've been once before with John Lawton when he left Half Way House, so I know it's good."

Annie made sure she wore her best outfit to work on the following Saturday and her brown Woolworth's coverall kept it clean while she was working. When she finished work at five-thirty, she changed into her black patent leather shoes with sling backs and kitten heels. When Margot saw Annie in a white mini skirt and crocheted black top, she gave her a hug and said, "My word, you do look bonny, Annie. I love black and white. Always looks nice, especially with your fair hair. Don't tell me you're going on a date."

Annie grinned. "All right, I won't tell you I'm going on a date," she said laughing with her supervisor.

"Well, you enjoy yourself and don't do anything I wouldn't do!" Margot advised.

"I don't know what you wouldn't do, Margot, so I'll just use my instincts," Annie replied.

David was waiting for her on the corner of Bridge Street when she came out of work. He too had spruced up and Annie smiled as she approached him.

"You look lovely, Annie," he told her. "I've never seen you in your Sunday best, or your Saturday best either."

"You're not so bad yourself," she said. "I've never seen you in your Saturday best either."

He took her hand and this time she didn't snatch it away. The late afternoon sun was warm and everybody was dressed appropriately for the balmy summer evening. Girls in summer dresses and boys in Chinos or Farah pants and short sleeved shirts gave the town a holiday atmosphere. They arrived at the restaurant as they were just opening for evening meals. Several people were waiting outside.

"It looks like we aren't the only ones having an early dinner," David observed. "Maybe they're going to see Elvis like we are."

After they'd had dinner, they had enough time to wander hand-in-hand round to the Odeon without fear of missing the beginning of the programme.

"I'm really looking forward to this," Annie said excitedly.

"I know you'll love it," David told her. "There are other things that come on before the main feature film starts."

"Oooh!" Annie exclaimed. "What sort of things?"

"Well, usually there's the Pathé news and a cartoon...something like Tom and Jerry or Woody Woodpecker. We'll also get trailers for films that are due to be shown at a later date."

"Sounds good," Annie enthused.

"Yeah...but it's frustrating sometimes because all you want to see is the main feature," David explained. "But maybe I'm just impatient."

When they arrived at the Odeon, there were long queues of people waiting to get in. Annie and David joined the queue for the rear circle and when they got inside, Annie was fascinated with the decorative opulence of the theatre. "This is beautiful," she said in awe. "I would never have imagined anything like this."

David had bought the tickets for two rear circle seats: one shilling and sixpence each.

"Shall I pay for the tickets, David?" Annie asked. "You paid for dinner so it's only fair."

"Thanks for offering, Annie, but it's a gentleman's privilege to pay for everything on a first date," he told her. "That's just the way it is."

"Well, thank you, but..."

"No buts, Miss O'Shea," he said firmly. "This is all my shout."

He handed the tickets to the usherette on the door and she tore them in half, keeping one half and returning the other half to David. He led Annie up the steps to the back row of the rear circle. "Why are we going right to the back?" she asked.

"We'll be able to see better from up here," David said, trying to sound convincing.

"Okay," Annie replied, happy to bow to David's superior knowledge.

Almost as soon as they settled in their seats, the lights went down and the rich red velvet curtains opened to reveal an enormous screen. Annie felt a thrill course through her whole body and David took her hand, squeezing it gently. As David had said earlier, the Pathé news came on first and it revealed all sorts of stuff that was going on in the world. Nikita Khrushchev had pounded his shoe on the table at a United Nations General Assembly meeting, protesting the discussion of Soviet Union policy toward Eastern Europe; Britain had test-launched the Polaris missile and France tested its first atomic bomb in the Sahara desert.

"This is all very serious and scary, isn't it?" Annie whispered. David nodded, but didn't answer and confidently placed his arm around Annie's shoulders as they watched more light-hearted news which informed them that a group called The Beatles had gone to perform in a club in Hamburg and a guy called Cliff Richard was supposed to be Britain's answer to Elvis Presley.

Annie's eyes slowly became used to the darkness and she was able to see couples in each other's arms almost everywhere in the rear circle and nobody seemed to mind. Instinctively, she leaned in towards David, who adjusted his position to accommodate Annie's tiny frame. She rested her head on his shoulder, sitting up only to laugh at the antics of Wile E Coyote and the Road Runner. As the cartoon finished, David turned her face to his and kissed her gently. Realising Annie had not objected, he kissed her, again holding her face in his hands and covering her lips with his mouth.

Annie tensed at first, but then relaxed as her whole body felt as though she were floating on air. She closed her eyes and enjoyed the moment. *Now I know what Bella was going on about,* she thought. *And what did Margot say? Go with the flow.* She intuitively parted her lips and felt his tongue find its way through to hers. David pulled away momentarily. He took a deep breath and whispered, "Annie O'Shea, I'm crazy about you," and he kissed her again, feeling the love that was making his heart leap and his head spin with passion. He took another deep breath as the lights came up and couples parted as if on cue, adjusting hair and clothing and making themselves respectable for public view.

During the intermission, a lady with a refrigerated tray appeared in the aisle selling ice cream and Lions Maid orange ice lollies. "Would you like a tub or a choc ice?" David asked.

"I'd love one of those orange lollies, please," she said.

"Your wish is my command," he replied with a flourish and he skipped down the steps to the lady who stood in the passageway between the rear circle and the dress circle.

As David came back up the stairs with the lolly Annie had requested and a choc ice for himself, she noticed, not for the first time, how handsome he was. His skin was tanned from the sun and his dark hair, slightly curly, was cut so as not to rest on his collar, but not to look like the crew cuts some of the boys at Half Way House had. He didn't part his hair and it was combed back with a modest quiff at the front. *Hmm,* she thought, *I am one lucky girl to have David as my boyfriend.* She paused her thoughts to keep herself in check. *What girl wouldn't love to be going out with him? Slow down, Annie. This is your first date and you aren't sure how much you should tell him... but he did say he was crazy about me, didn't he?*

When the lights went down again, boys' arms went round their girls again and in the half light, it was clear when passion took over. When Elvis sang *Tonight is so right for love,* David kissed Annie and they listened to the words as their lips came together. For them, that night was indeed so right for love and they were both in a place where they were comfortable and happy.

They went on the upper deck of the bus going home and sat on the back seat where they were out of view of the conductor and anybody else who sat in front of them. "I can see why girls like Elvis Presley," Annie said pensively. "I'm not sure I could fall in love with him, but he has plenty of qualities that a lot of girls like. Thanks for taking me, David. I can join in conversations at work now."

"My pleasure, Annie," he replied as he placed his arm around her again, "but I hope you got more out of it than information for a topic of conversation at work."

She turned to face him, looked him straight in the eye and said, "Well, you have opened my mind to the wonders of ..." She paused and then coyly continued, "... to the wonders of film and of Elvis Presley."

David looked crushed. "Oh," was all he could say.

"And..." she continued, "...to the wonderful feeling when you are kissed by a boy who says he's crazy about you."

David smiled. "Phew," he said in relief. "I thought I had offended you again, but if I had, you sure didn't show it and in the words of the new Elvis Presley hit, I really can't help falling in love with you, Annie O'Shea."

Annie was taken aback when the word *love* entered the equation. "Oh, I see," she said, uncertain how she should react. "I don't know what love is yet, but if tonight is anything to go by, I think I like it."

David looked sad. "Aw, Annie, haven't you ever experienced love of any kind?" he asked tenderly.

"I don't know," she answered honestly. "One of my first memories was from when Bella was given the task of looking after me very soon after I was found on the doorstep of St Anthony's. I told her I loved her and she shot me down in flames...metaphorically speaking, of course."

"Well, maybe you remembered somebody saying it to you before you arrived at St Anthony's," David suggested.

"Who knows?"

"Have you ever thought of trying to find the woman who gave birth to you?" David asked. "I mean, there must be a birth certificate somewhere."

Annie shook her head. "The nuns always told us we should accept our lot and not wonder where our parents were, because we might uncover things we didn't want to know and it's better not to look back but to look to the future. Now you've brought it up, though, I might be interested. Once I've qualified and settled into nursing, I might think about it then."

When they arrived back at Half Way House, they kissed goodnight before they went inside. Mrs Constable was in the entrance hall checking the signing out/signing in book and as they went in together, she looked surprised. "Have you two been out together?" she questioned.

"We went to the Odeon to see Elvis Presley," David told her.

"Together?" Mrs Constable asked again.

"Well, yes, together," David said. "That's all right, isn't it, Mrs Constable?"

Mrs Constable looked perplexed. "Well, that depends on whether you went just as friends, or you went as something more than friends. You understand what I am saying, don't you?"

Alarms rang in David's head. *I must protect Annie's reputation.* "We are just friends, Mrs Constable."

"Good," the woman said firmly. "I am responsible for your well-being and we cannot cope with unsavoury happenings between boys and girls, can we?"

Annie and David shook their heads in dumb silence and then in unison, "Goodnight, Mrs Constable.

As they went upstairs, Annie whispered to David that Bella had had similar questioning one night when she had been out with Jack. "Thanks for coming to the rescue. I don't know what her problem is."

"Maybe she had something happen to her as a teenager, but don't worry, we'll be very discreet," David said quietly as they reached the landing where Annie had to turn right and David had to climb the rest of the stairs to the Top East corridor. "Goodnight, Annie," he whispered and winked at her knowingly.

"Goodnight, David," she murmured and then giving him the most genuine smile, "Thank you for tonight."

Seven

Bella and Jack went to view several rental flats and houses in Horwich and Rivington, but found nothing suitable. Bella was becoming despondent. "I'm fed up," she whined. "I thought it would be easy finding a flat. Mrs Constable told me to put my name on the Council housing list, but I could be waiting ages and it might not be where I want to live."

Jack agreed. "I'm disappointed for you, love, but why don't I take you home to meet my parents? They might have some suggestions."

Bella was shocked. "Bloody..." She stopped abruptly and tempered her language. "Blimey, Jack, are you sure you want them to meet me? Do they know I'm an orphan? Do they know I was brought up by nuns? Do they..."

"Stop it, Bella," Jack interrupted. "They know I've been seeing a girl from work who lives in Rivington, but that's all. I didn't think it necessary to tell them your life history..."

"...such as it is." Bella completed his sentence.

"No, I didn't mean that and this is me you are talking to, Bella, not a complete stranger. Don't be going all defensive on me again. I thought we'd got over all that stuff."

"We have, but I never asked about your parents because I have none. I'm not sure why you haven't mentioned them to me before, or told me where you live, but to be honest, I'm not really concerned about that." Bella was gabbling. "I know what people think about orphanage girls. They think we know nothing and..."

"What do you mean?" Jack asked.

"I mean," Bella said resolutely, "that when we went to Mass on Sundays, all dressed in our brown coats and brown berets, neat white ankle-socks on our feet in brown lace-up shoes, we could feel and often hear words of pity and derision as well as kids sniggering and pointing when we were made to walk in line and not speak to anybody. That was hard for me, because back then, I said what I thought even when I knew I would be punished for it. I once told a woman to go to hell and the Mother Superior put me in isolation for a week as my penance."

Jack was stunned. "I'm so sorry, love, but I don't think my mum and dad would think badly of you..."

"But you've not told them about me, have you?"

"No, I haven't, but not because I'm ashamed of you. On the contrary. I'm proud of you and I love it when other guys look at you with admiration in their eyes, because I'm the one you love and *I* love you too. I didn't want my mum and dad to hassle me until I was ready to take the next step."

Bella cocked her head to one side. "Why are you taking me to meet them now and what's this next step you are taking?" she asked, still with tension in her voice.

"It just seems like the right time," Jack told her. He paused and then suddenly out of the blue said, "Will you marry me, Bella?"

"What?"

"Do I need to ask you again? I want to marry you and make an honest woman of you," Jack beamed. "Well, will you?"

Bella was in shock. "Can I think about it?"

Jack was disappointed. "If you have to, but don't keep me waiting too long. I have an ulterior motive for asking you and I need to organise something if you say yes. Please, Bella, don't leave me dangling on a string."

Bella looked at him and saw the confusion in his eyes. "I'll try not to, but for me it's a massive step to take."

"And you think it isn't a massive step for me too?" Jack demanded.

Bella tried to stop herself from becoming irritated. "I'm sure it is, Jack, but you have parents who have shown you what marriage is all about. They have set the example. All I have had is a group of nuns who are married to God, and I'm not saying there's anything wrong with that, because it's their choice, but it's not like marriage in the real world, is it?"

"Okay, if that's the way you want it, I'll give you until this weekend and then only you can decide what you want." Jack was demoralised and it showed.

~ * ~

Annie and Bella met up in Bolton at lunchtime the following day. Annie noticed Bella's morose mood as they sat in the Casa Blanca coffee bar near Bolton Town Hall and asked if she might do anything to help. "You have been so happy for months, Bella. What has happened to make you feel so miserable?"

Bella shrugged. "I'm not sure I can explain it to you, Annie. I feel like I have the worries of the world on my shoulders."

"Why?" Annie asked sympathetically. "You haven't split up with Jack, have you?"

"On the contrary," Bella told her. "He's asked me to marry him and he wants me to meet his parents."

Annie was overjoyed. "Bella, that's wonderful! Why would you be sad about something like that? It's the magic that has been waiting for you; the magic we could only dream about before! What is it that's worrying you?"

"Marriage is worrying me, Annie. Marriage with a big fat capital M."

"But why?" Annie pressed.

Bella sighed deeply. "I have no idea what it's all about, Annie, and I'm scared. I love Jack and I know he loves me, but is that enough?"

"It should be, shouldn't it?" Annie urged. "I think if David..."

Bella suddenly came to life. "David?" she shrieked. "You and David Anderson? Annie O'Shea! You little tinker! Why didn't you tell me? You've kept that quiet, haven't you?"

Annie looked sheepish. "We were almost caught out by Mrs Constable after our first date... remember how she questioned you about your smudged lipstick? Well, we made a conscious decision to hide our relationship, so it has been a well-kept secret."

"But you could have told me, Annie. Since when have you kept secrets from me?" Bella asked, somewhat deflated.

"Since I went out with David, that's all," Annie told her, "and it might sound silly, but I didn't want to share the happiness with anybody, Bella. I know that's selfish, but it's the first time I have experienced those feelings and they are *my* feelings, not for anybody else."

"But I shared my feelings with you, didn't I?" Bella muttered. "I told you when we had been kissing and cuddling in the car..." She stopped abruptly on realising she had not told Annie the whole story. "Well, never mind. I understand, honest I do, but to get back to my problem, what am I going to tell Jack? He won't wait for my answer forever."

"I guess you have to go with your heart, Bella," Annie advised cautiously, "but with something as massive as marriage, I would think you have to be sure in your mind that it's the right thing to do."

Bella was perplexed. "Well, you're a fat lot of help, Annie! My heart says I love him, but it's my head that's causing the problem." She hesitated. "Maybe I should just chop off my head and the problem would be solved."

"Now you're being melodramatic," Annie scolded. "Would it help to talk to Sister Agatha? She usually had a more down-to-earth approach than the other nuns."

"And now *you* are being downright silly," Bella retorted. "She'll just tell me to pray, but I've already done that and I didn't get an answer."

Annie looked at her watch. "Goodness, it's almost half past one. I'd better get back to tech. I have my second maths paper in half an hour."

As they left the coffee bar, Bella gave Annie a hug. "Thanks for listening to me, Annie. I don't know what I'd do without you. Will you be my bridesmaid?"

Annie whooped with joy. "So you've decided then?"

Bella nodded. "I can think of a lot worse things that could happen to me and I know Jack loves me. All you need is love, eh? I guess I have made my decision."

~ * ~

Annie happily went back to college after Bella had told her she was going to marry Jack. She sailed through her maths exam and looked forward to seeing David after school. She had arranged to meet him at Moor Lane bus station so they might take the Rivington bus together. When she arrived there, David was sitting on a bench patiently waiting.

"Have you been here long?" she asked as she gave him a welcome kiss on the cheek.

"About fifteen minutes," he answered. "I had a study period at the end of the afternoon so I sneaked out a few minutes early so I wouldn't have to join the queue of marauding school kids on Bradshaw Road."

"Oooh, what a snob!" she teased. "Just a few years ago, you were one of those marauding kids yourself."

"Touché, Miss O'Shea," he responded. "In that respect, you have the upper hand."

"How do you mean?" she asked. "Being at an orphanage school wasn't ideal. In fact, I think I would have preferred to be a marauding kid going to a stable family home for my tea."

"Whoops," David said. "Sorry if I touched a nerve, and for the record, I didn't have a stable home to go to at that time, but no offence meant."

She smiled. "None taken, but I have some fabulous news. Bella and Jack are going to get married!"

"Wow! When did all this happen?"

"Yesterday, I think," Annie told him. "I met Bella at lunchtime and she was very worried about the whole marriage thing. After we'd talked it through, she decided it was the best thing that has ever happened to her. She's going to tell Jack tomorrow. I'm so excited for her and she's asked me to be bridesmaid."

On the way back, Annie and David held hands and cuddled on the upper deck of the bus, but as soon as they were in sight of Half Way House, they separated and walked down the drive several yards apart so as not to give Mrs Constable the wrong idea.

At breakfast the following morning, Annie sat with Bella and David sat with the other boys so as not to arouse suspicion. Bella commented on the situation. "How can you bear not to be near him all the time, Annie? I hate being away from Jack."

Annie looked at her friend and said, "Just think, you'll be with him twenty-four hours a day when you are married and think of all the rest that goes with being married." She pressed her lips together and raised her eyebrows subtly.

"Annie O'Shea," Bella whispered with dramatic intent. "Wash your mouth out with soap and water! Who says I haven't done that already?"

Now it was Annie's turn to be dramatic. "Excuse me?" she whispered as loud as she dared. "Have you, Bella? Have you really?"

Bella took a deep breath and said coyly, "I have, Annie. I wouldn't spin you a yarn about that. I think Mrs Constable knew what we'd been doing when she caught me coming in that night. When you love somebody, you just have to do it. Haven't you and David done it?"

"No, we haven't and we don't intend to, not that we've ever discussed it," Annie said with conviction. "David wants to go to university and I have my nursing training to do. We're in the middle of our exams so all our time is spent studying. The possible consequences would be too great if we had sex."

"Don't say it like that, Annie," Bella objected. "Sex sounds dirty; making love is exactly that, fulfilling your love. Jack told me it was the absolute epitome of showing how much we loved each other and Annie, Annie, Annie, it didn't seem wrong." She was beginning to get excited as she continued, "I wanted to show him how much I love him. It's nothing like the nuns would have us believe. It's a feeling that's indescribable. You feel it though your whole body and it takes your breath away, but at the same time, you are breathing from the bottom of your soul whilst you are floating on a cloud somewhere outside of your body.”

Annie was totally shocked. “Hell’s teeth, Bella! It’s hard to believe you are so eloquent about it! But what if you get pregnant?” she asked earnestly. “Your life as you know it would be over.”

“No it wouldn’t,” Bella corrected. “My life would begin and I could lavish my child with all the love and affection I missed out on. Surely you can understand that.”

Annie smiled. “Of course I understand that, but you are young and you need to get used to living independently before you tie yourself down with children.”

“I know, Annie, but I can’t wait now to be a wife and a mother,” Bella disclosed. “I’m actually looking forward to going to work tonight and telling Jack. I’ll tell you how it goes at breakfast tomorrow. Jack and I are both on the late shift tonight.”

Annie pondered for a moment. “So why were you so uncertain about marriage if you’ve already taken the biggest step in that direction? I thought that was what was bothering you.”

“No, *that* wasn’t bothering me at all. I know I am going to enjoy that side of marriage, but it’s all the other stuff like housekeeping, cooking, bills, mortgage...you name it and it’s what married life is all about,” Bella told her. “How will I cope with all of that and still have time to enjoy all the things I have recently discovered? It’s scary, Annie.”

Annie took hold of Bella’s hand and squeezed it affectionately. “There’ll be two of you and you’ll help each other. That’s what I understand marriage to be about...caring and sharing.”

“I know you’re right and here I am taking advice from you,” Bella said. “I wouldn’t have done that a few years ago, would I?”

“No, you wouldn’t,” Annie agreed, “but you have changed so much since you met Jack. You have mellowed and nobody appreciates that more than I do. You go to work tonight and give him your answer. He’ll be over the moon.”

Eight

When Bella went into work that evening, Jack was not behind the bar. Rick was there and he nodded to her as she busied herself at her station in preparation for the evening meals. Her shift was hectic and she was silently grateful that she hadn't had time to worry about her private life, that was, until the end of the shift.

"Where's Jack?" she asked Rick.

"I thought you'd know," Rick said. "He just hasn't turned in tonight."

Bella looked worried. "I have no idea where he is," she told Rick. "It's probably a good job Mr Winters is on his day off... otherwise there would have been hell to pay."

Rick shrugged. "I've never known Jack not to turn up for work when he's rostered on. Can you go round to his place in the morning and ask if he's coming in tomorrow? Winters will be on his case if he doesn't turn up again."

Bella felt her face burning.

"What's up?" Rick asked. "Have I said the wrong thing? Have you two split up or something?"

Bella shook her head vigorously. "No, we haven't, at least I don't think we have," she said in her confusion. "We had a bit of a disagreement last night, but nothing I can't handle. The truth is, I don't know where he lives."

Rick looked puzzled. "You don't know where he lives?" he asked, disbelieving. "Don't be daft, Bella. You've been going out with him for almost two years and you don't know where he lives? Pull the other one, there's bells on it!"

Bella blushed again. "No, I don't know where he lives; I never asked and he never told me. When you are an orphan, Rick, you don't ask for details of loving homes and caring parents."

"Sorry," Rick said. "I didn't know. I just assumed you lived with your parents... sorry. If I give you his address, do you think you could go round to see him in tomorrow? I'd go, but I'm taking my wife to the doctor's at ten thirty and then coming straight here for my shift."

Bella breathed in deeply. *What do I do?* she thought. *I can't just turn up unannounced, can I? Jack might not want to see me and that's why he didn't come to work tonight. Please God, tell me what I should do.* "Okay," she offered. "I'll go round in the morning."

Rick took a paper napkin from the bar and wrote: *The White House, Chorley New Road.* "It's just after the golf club, set back from the road. You can get the bus from Greenhough Lane. They run every half hour...ten past and twenty to. I just hope he's all right. Not like him at all to be off work."

~ * ~

Bella took the twenty to ten bus and got off at the golf club. She walked back about a hundred yards until she came to the driveway of Jack's house—*The White House*—and felt sick. *No wonder he didn't bring me here,* she thought. *He lives in a mansion! How would I fit in with all this wealth? I'm an orphan who has absolutely nothing by comparison. My few hundred pounds in the bank is my worldly wealth. His parents will think I'm going out with him for his money. They'll hate me. How can I compete with them? They'll probably be snooty and look down their noses at me. Oh Jack, I can't marry you. How can I?*

She stood at the wrought iron gates for ages, going over and over the situation in her mind, wondering what she should do. She went to the kerb, checked there were no cars on the wide road, stepped off with one foot and then pulled back abruptly. *What are you doing, Bella Jones? Where's that strong girl who left St Anthony's full of confidence and afraid of nobody? You came to find out why Jack wasn't at work, so you will bloody well go up to the door and ring the bell. If Jack answers, it will be all right; if his mother answers, I can deal with a woman; if his dad answers, I'll just stand my ground. What can they do? They're not going to kill me, are they?*

She pressed down the latch on the gate and it opened with a screech. Gritting her teeth, she marched purposefully to the door. Her emotions were playing games... confident then timid; anxious then calm. Tentatively, she rang the bell and heard the chimes ring out inside. Nobody came to the door and she rang again.

"Coming."

It was Jack's voice and she breathed a sigh of relief. She heard the bolt being drawn and she prepared herself for coming face to face with Jack. When the door opened, she was shocked when a fresh-faced young man appeared and she stood there, gaping at the person who was supposed to be Jack, but who wasn't.

"Hello," the young man said amicably. "What can I do for you?"

"Er," Bella faltered. "Er... I'm looking for Jack Spencer. Does he live here?"

"He does and who are you?" he asked with a twinkle in his eye.

"She's Bella Jones and she's with me, James Spencer. Hello, Bella. This is my brother, James." Jack had crept up behind James and pushed him out of the way. "I'll take it from here, little brother. Off you go now and play with your toys!"

"Well, hello, Bella. Nice to meet you," James said as he turned to go back inside. "It's a pity you didn't meet me first. I'm much better looking than him. Make sure he treats you right and if he doesn't, you know where I am."

"On your bike, James, and stop showing off." Jack spoke with an older brother's authority and it struck a chord with Bella.

Maybe that's how I was with Annie…telling her off all the time and thinking I knew better than her. Perhaps that's how siblings treat each other.

"What are you doing here, Bella?" Jack asked. "I would never have thought you would come here on your own."

"You didn't give us much choice," she told him firmly. "You didn't turn up at work yesterday and Rick had to do the work of two men. Mr Winters wasn't in so at least that let's you off the hook with him. Are you going to ask me in or do I have talk to you on the doorstep like a hawker?"

Jack apologised. "I'm sorry I let everybody down and please come in. We'll go in the breakfast room. Can I make you a coffee?"

The atmosphere was strained and Bella felt uncomfortable. "Yes please," she said and she awkwardly took a seat at the small table, placing her handbag on the table in front of her.

"How did you find out where I live?" Jack called from the kitchen.

"Rick told me."

"Oh."

Jack returned with two cups and sat at the table across from Bella. She nervously held her cup with both hands and looked down as she took a sip.

"Have you come to give me your answer?" he asked earnestly.

Bella looked at the young man she loved with all her heart and yet felt she would not be able to articulate what she was thinking. "Actually, I came to see if you were coming to work tonight, because Rick says he can't manage on his own and the temporary barman has found another job. Rick couldn't come himself because he's taking his wife to a hospital appointment."

"Couldn't he have phoned?" Jack asked non-commitally.

"He didn't say he had your number so I can't answer that," Bella said feeling herself becoming distressed with their attempts at small talk. "Are you going to tell me why you weren't at work last night?"

"Not until you give me your answer to what I asked you a couple of days ago," he said seriously.

Bella desperately tried to calm herself before she spoke. "I did intend telling you I would marry you..."

Jack's heart was pounding in his chest. "Am I right in suspecting there's a *but* coming?" he asked with trepidation.

"I love you, Jack, but now that I've seen where you live, I don't think I could go through with it."

"Why?" Jack's voice broke with anxiety.

"Look at all this," she said as she waved her hand around the room which, to her, was luxurious in the extreme. "I could never fit into these surroundings. I'm an orphan; I don't know what my background is other than I'm half Italian. I was brought up by nuns who instilled over-the-top morals into me and I rebelled all the time because I wanted affection from women who didn't really know how to give it. How can I be a normal wife if I feel uncomfortable in my surroundings?"

"But surely you can leave all that behind now," Jack reasoned. "I thought our love was strong enough to overcome your hang-ups with your past."

"I *am* moving on, very slowly though," she told him, "but you are my first boyfriend, my first lover and I'm not sure that I should marry the first boy who has paid me attention."

Jack looked at her in bewilderment. "For Christ's sake, Bella, what are you saying?"

"Don't take the Lord's name in vain," Bella interjected. "You'll end up in hellfire and damnation."

Jack was becoming more and more agitated. "Don't preach your Catholic morals to me, Bella. I'm not a bad person, even though I don't go to church and I don't need your sanctimonious attitude just now. I'm beginning to think I shouldn't have asked you to marry me in the first place. Just forget I ever asked and go back to your naïve little life."

Bella felt hot tears trickling down her cheeks. "I can't believe you are saying that," she sobbed. "I thought you loved me, truly loved me. Now I'm wondering if you are treating me like those willing girls you talked about when we first made love."

Jack stared at her, his eyes wild with anger. He threw up his arms in disgust and opened the door, signalling to Bella that she should leave.

Bella stood up quickly and instinctively stepped back to avoid Jack's flailing arms. "Will you be at work tonight?" she managed to ask.

"No," he snapped. "I'll phone in; don't you worry your pretty little head about it. Goodbye, Bella. It was nice..." He didn't finish his sentence.

With Jack's words ringing in her ears, Bella snatched her handbag from the table and ran through the open door, straight down the drive and onto the road. Jack slammed the door in her wake and didn't hear the screeching of brakes and the sickening thud as the van hit the girl, carrying her limp body several yards along Chorley New Road.

Nine

Annie missed Bella that morning. She had arranged to have an early breakfast so she could catch the early bus into Bolton with David. He had his final A level exam and had to be in school by eight-thirty in order to find his place in the examination centre and have time to compose himself before the start of the three hour paper.

They parted ways at Moor Lane and she kissed him on the cheek. "Good luck," she said and hugged him tightly. "I'll be thinking of you. I'm sure you'll smash it if your revision is anything to go by."

"Thanks, baby," David said and ran off to catch the Bradshaw bus just as it was leaving. Blowing a kiss to Annie as she waved him off from the bus stop, he mouthed, *"Love you."*

"Love you too," she mouthed back and then went happily on her way.

Throughout out the day, her mind kept wandering away from differential and integral calculus in her maths revision and she found it hopeless trying to concentrate on trigonometric function. David's English literature exam kept invading her mind and then Bella's looming engagement interfered with her usual diligent focus on her studies. By the time the end-of-lessons bell rang, she breathed a sigh of relief. Her own exams had begun and she had already done

64

Chemistry, Maths paper one and Biology papers one and two and she knew she would have to make up the time she felt she had wasted by allowing herself to be distracted during her revision period.

She travelled home alone since David's exam finished at noon. It was four-thirty when she got off the bus at Greenhough Lane and she was pleasantly surprised to see David waiting for her at the bus stop. "Hi, babe!" she greeted him happily. "How did it go? Did you get the questions on *Macbeth* and *Yeats*, or did you get *Wordsworth's Prelude*? I hope you got what you'd revised for." Noticing how miserable David looked, she asked, "What's wrong, babe? Was the exam that bad? You look so sad. What is it?"

David stopped her in her tracks and took her in his arms. He held her tightly for what seemed a long time, but in reality was only a few seconds. Releasing his hold, he faced her and held her at arm's length. "It's Bella," he whispered. "She's had an accident."

Annie felt her face pale. "What... sort... of... an... accident?" she stammered.

David hugged her again, stoically trying to give her strength to deal with the news he was about to impart. "A road accident," he explained, "on Chorley New Road. She apparently ran onto the road without looking. The police have been at Half Way House most of the afternoon. I wanted to tell you before you saw the police car at the front door. Mrs Constable thought it would be best for me to give you the news."

"But Bella's going to be all right, isn't she?" she asked, her voice faltering as she spoke. "Can I go to see her? I'll just drop my things off and go straight to the hospital."

David looked down at his feet to hide his distress.

"David?" she questioned. "David?" Her voice came out as a high pitched whine.

He shook his head slowly as hot tears fell from his eyes. "Oh Annie, I don't know what to say. I'm so sorry," he sobbed. "So very, very sorry."

Annie stared into space. She didn't blink and just remained motionless staring somewhere between reality and nothingness.

Suddenly, she let out an almighty scream. "No," she cried. "No, no, no." And she fell to her knees in despair.

David knelt beside her until she had recovered enough to walk the next few steps to Half Way House.

~ * ~

Annie's final exam was the following day and she struggled to motivate herself. She had hardly slept and when she did drop off to sleep, she was haunted by pictures of Bella being dragged along the road like a rag doll.

"Can't you ask for a deferment, Annie?" Mrs Constable suggested.

"I don't know, but I've done all my revision so I think I'll try to focus just for one more day," Annie told her through her tears. "I can do it, Mrs C. I can do it for Bella."

"Well, if you're sure, Annie. Don't put too much pressure on yourself," the concerned woman advised.

"I'll do my best. I have to," Annie concluded and she brushed away her tears with the back of her hand. *Bella tried to make me strong so I'll do it for her. If I focus all my energy in getting through today, her strength of character will see me through, I'm sure.*

The following day, Mrs Constable noticed Annie had locked herself away in her room and had not eaten for twenty-four hours. She thought Annie had forced herself into denial about the accident in order to complete the final paper, but once the exams were over, the realisation of Bella's death would hit her with extreme severity. Knocking on the door of ME3, she called gently, "Annie? Are you all right? We have missed you. I have brought you a sandwich and a flask of coffee." Not hearing any response, she placed the plate and flask on the floor by the door. "I'll leave it here for you to have when you feel like it. Please remember that we are here if you need us." With that, Mrs Constable sighed and walked away, turning several times to see if Annie had opened her door to retrieve the food and drink, but it remained there untouched for several hours.

Inside the room, Annie was curled up on her bed, still in her pyjamas, her eyes red and swollen from all the tears she had shed for her dearest friend. When there was another knock on her door after darkness had flooded her room, she wanted to call out, *GO AWAY,* but when she heard David's voice, she stirred.

"Annie, it's me," he said quietly. "Please open the door."

"I can't see you just now, David. Just leave me alone."

"No, I won't leave without seeing you. You have to talk to me," David coaxed. "I'm worried about you."

Slowly, Annie stretched out her legs and pushed herself up. She caught sight of her reflection in the mirror and cringed at what she saw. Grabbing her dressing gown from inside the wardrobe, she slipped her arms into the sleeves and didn't bother to fasten the buttons. She shuffled across to the door and opened it slowly. When she saw David standing there, she burst into tears again.

"May I come in?" he asked.

She opened the door further and signalled to him that he might go into her room for the first time. She tried to smile, but failed in her attempts to show she was in control. "I'm sorry, David. I'm sorry," she cried.

David held her close and allowed her to weep into his chest. He stroked her hair that was damp and lank. "Just cry as much as you like, love. Let it all come out. That way, I'm sure you'll feel better."

Annie sniffed and wiped her face on her sleeve. "I have tried to be strong like Bella had taught me, but it's hard, David; it's so hard."

"You have to grieve, Annie, but you are not alone. You have to understand that everybody is here to help you through this very sad time. None of us can truly say we were as close to Bella as you were, but personally, I know I can try to share your grief and be here for you when you need me."

Annie went to sit on the bed. She looked sadly at the young man who had stolen her heart. "Please will you get my facecloth from the bathroom?" she asked.

David did as she asked and she wiped her face, feeling the coolness of the damp cloth ease her burning eyes. She patted the bed next to her signalling to David that she wanted him to sit by her. Uncertain about it, David cautiously went to sit by her. Out of the blue, Annie asked, "Will you make love to me?"

David was taken aback. "Annie," he said gently. "Do you know what you are asking? It's every boy's dream to make love to his girlfriend and I'd be a liar if I said I hadn't thought about it each time I kissed you, but is this the right time? I mean, it's not that I don't love you, but..."

"I know Bella wanted me to do it. She described to me how wonderful making love is," she told him quietly. "I think I will feel closer to Bella if I can float on that cloud of love like she explained."

David was completely baffled. "I have never slept with a girl," he said bluntly. "How do I know I'll be able to transport you to those heights like Bella described? I don't want to be a disappointment to you, Annie."

"Love me, David, please," she implored. She removed her pyjamas and slipped between the sheets. She looked at him longingly.

"If you're sure, Annie." He slowly removed his clothes, feeling very self-conscious in his nakedness, even though the room was dark and he slipped into bed with the girl to whom he had declared his love on more than one occasion.

Annie snuggled up to him and felt the skin on skin she had always been instructed to avoid. She held David's head in her hands and kissed him lovingly, urgently, desperately.

David tensed. "I can't do it, Annie. It's the wrong time and we aren't doing it for the right reasons. Grief is not a reason to make love."

"But Bella would expect us to carry on as normal, David. I know she would."

David slid out of the bed and hastily put on his clothes. "This isn't normal for us, is it?" He was embarrassed and he was unable to hide how he was feeling. "My friends at school would never believe I have been in bed with a naked girl and not touched her. I could never admit that to anybody. I feel stupid and I shouldn't have led you to believe I *could* make love to you. I'm sorry, Annie."

Annie rested her head on her pillow and looked particularly beautiful to David as she whispered, "I'm sorry. I should never have asked. Somehow, I thought that experiencing what Bella had experienced might help me cope with losing her." Tears that had become commonplace during the past twenty-four hours trickled down her cheeks. "I do understand and I hope this won't harm our relationship. Please don't hate me. I couldn't bear to lose you too."

David felt awkward. "We have a lot to contend with in the next week or so," he said, trying to regain his equanimity. "Do you think we can forget today and get on with what we have to do?"

Annie sat up, making sure she covered herself with the sheet. "I'm so sorry, David. I didn't mean to embarrass you." She paused and looked directly at the boy she loved with all her heart. "You'll not believe this, but I think my rash actions seem to have actually brought a bit of normality back into my life. I might get up now and shower to make myself feel respectable. I still have an aching deep in my heart that feels like it will be there for ever, but I'll manage to pull through with your help if you are still prepared to give it."

"I think the aching will go with time, Annie, and yes, I shall be here for you always," David replied honestly. "I'll leave you to sort yourself out and I'll see you at breakfast in the morning." He pecked her on the cheek and said, "Goodnight, Annie. Sleep well."

~ * ~

Next morning, David called for Annie on the way down to the dining room. She looked brighter than the night before, but she appeared quiet and pensive as she opened her door.

"How are you feeling?" David asked.

"I'll be fine," she assured him. "I'll have to be. Thank you for last night."

"Not a problem," he said as he smiled to hide his true feelings. *I can't believe I was such a wimp, but I still feel it wasn't the right time to go the whole way. I'll just have to live with what I didn't do and hope Annie understands.*

The next few days were spent trying to understand what might have happened to Belle. There was going to be an inquest, but the driver of the van that had hit Belle on Chorley New Road was the only witness. The report in the *Bolton Evening News* said: '*she had run from the drive of The White House belonging to Mr and Mrs John James Spencer, local real estate agents, who do not know the girl.*

It was unclear why she had been there and the police were making enquiries...'

"They must be Jack's parents," Annie said as she closed the newspaper. "I wonder why Jack's name wasn't mentioned."

"Maybe Bella was going to see him," David suggested.

"She was going to tell Jack she would marry him the night before and he was going to introduce her to his parents," Annie explained. "She was nervous about it for some reason and I can't imagine her going to his house without him. If Jack's parents have said they didn't know her, the whole scenario must never have happened."

Mrs Constable came into the drawing room. "How are you, Annie? We are all in shock. Mother Superior and Sister Agatha went to identify Bella this morning. The Coroner is going to issue an interim death certificate so that we can arrange for the funeral Mass. Sister Agatha thought you might like to give the eulogy, Annie."

Annie's eyes were still red from all the weeping she had done since she had heard of the passing of her best friend and she fought to prevent the tears coming again as she spoke. "Of course I would love to give the eulogy, Mrs Constable. She was my sister in every way except we didn't have the same parents." She brushed away the stray tears that trickled down her face and she sobbed into her hands. David put his arm around her to comfort her and she rested her head on his shoulder. "You'll come to the funeral with me, won't you, David?"

David looked at Mrs Constable. "Am I allowed to attend, Mrs Constable? I'm not a Catholic, as you know."

"Of course, David," Mrs Constable told him. "Anybody may attend a requiem, but you won't be able to take Holy Communion."

"Even though I've been confirmed?" David asked.

"I'm afraid Christian unity has not yet come so far. The issue of transubstantiation always seems to be the stumbling block. Whether or not it will happen in the future, I don't know, but this is not the time nor place to be discussing religious issues. I do tend to get on my high horse when Christian unity is mentioned." She smiled and patted David on the shoulder. "Please do attend the funeral. Annie needs a friend to be there with her."

A week later, the funeral service was held in St Joseph's Church in Anderton where the girls of St Anthony's orphanage attended Mass regularly and they lined the driveway to the church door as the pallbearers bore the white coffin into the church. Annie and David were the first of the mourners followed by most of the nuns from St Anthony's and then Mrs Constable with the housemates. In the back pews of the church were two young men and several girls in black and white waitress uniforms and finally a middle aged gentleman. All bowed their heads as the funeral party entered the church.

Annie wept throughout the Mass and David held her hand to let her know she wasn't alone. When she was invited to give the eulogy, she stood and then paused to compose herself. Her thoughts were directed at Bella. *I can do this for you, Bella. I am going to show you how strong I have become. I know this is the last thing I will ever do for you and you deserve the best.* Slowly, she walked to the chancel steps and turned to face the congregation. She took a deep breath and began: *Bella Jones was the nearest person I had to a blood relative. She guided me through life's journey, always making sure I had everything she thought I needed...physically and emotionally.* Annie managed a little smile. *She often guided me into situations where, in all honesty, I should not have been, but always for the right reasons, her love and loyalty to me. I remember when I first arrived at St Anthony's, she took me into the convent orchard and we ate windfalls...well, Bella did. I was very small and didn't like the sour apples, but Bella was convinced those apples would subsidise our dinner and help fill our stomachs. I know she suffered a terrible tummy upset that night, but looking back, I don't think she ever ate Bramley apples again!*

Sometimes her confident manner was interpreted as boldness and disrespect, but she was convinced that she was alone in this world and nobody would stand up for her if she didn't do it for herself. More recently, she had found somebody who loved her and her whole personality changed. She ceased to be critical of everything around her and she began to see the positives in her life. I used to tell her that we should all have dreams and ambitions, a little bit of magic in our lives, and she frequently told me that waving a magic wand wouldn't change our lot. Had she dared to dream, I'm sure she would have had a more peaceful existence. However, I believe she found that magic in the person with whom she had fallen in love and it makes me very, very sad that she will no longer have the experience of loving and of being loved. Annie brushed away the tears as her voice faltered. *I shall miss Bella terribly for the rest of my life and I shall always remember her love and loyalty to me and take strength from her memory. Rest in peace, my dear sister, knowing that you loved and were loved. Thank you for being in my life.*

Returning to her seat next to David, she felt relieved that she had managed to open up her heart and share her best friend's loyalty with those present in the church.

"Well done, babe," David whispered and squeezed her hand. "I'm proud of you."

At the back of the church, a young man in a grey suit, immaculate white shirt and black tie, stood and called out, "May I say something, please?"

The priest in charge beckoned to him to come forward. "You are welcome to say a few words," he told the young man.

Standing at the steps, he faced the congregation and spoke confidently. "My name is Jack Spencer," he said. "I am the man who loved Bella and I loved her with all my heart. I asked her to marry me and although I believe she loved me, she found it difficult to leave her poor past behind to live in a more affluent world which seemed totally alien to her. She was confused the day that ..." he paused. "... the day when she ran from my house and..." Jack's confident voice disappeared and he coughed to recover his composure. "If I could bring her back, I would do it in a heartbeat. My love for Bella will never change. She brought sunshine into my life and I hope I brought sunshine into hers. There will forever be another bright star in the sky shining down on us all. Thank you for allowing me to share my grief with you all and thank you, Bella, for coming into my life. Rest in peace, my darling girl."

After the interment at the tiny cemetery at St Anthony's convent, the nuns invited everybody back to the refectory for light refreshment. The atmosphere was very subdued and sombre until Sister Agatha announced, as she tapped in the table to gain everybody's attention, "Good people, I know our Bella Jones wouldn't want us to be sad, so please feel free to make a little noise—Bella was never quiet—so I think it would be fitting for us all to share our memories with each other." She went to the Dansette record player in the corner and put an LP record on the turntable. "I think a little bit of music will lighten our load," she said and to the strains of *Danny Boy, I Believe* and *The Sound of Silence* by the popular Irish group, The Bachelors, spirits lifted and people began to form groups to talk to each other.

Annie and David went to talk to Jack and his friend whom they learned was Rick from Pike House Hotel. Jack and Rick had kept a low profile at the interment and also when they entered the refectory, so Annie thought she would like to speak to the young man to whom she had never formally been introduced.

"I'm Annie and this is David," she said as she offered her hand.

"May I give you a hug?" Jack asked. "Bella told me you were her closest friend and I never got the chance to say goodbye to her." He hugged her tightly and whispered, "I truly loved her, Annie. I wish I could turn the clock back and handle the proposal thing differently."

Annie pulled away from him and said, "Let's go for a walk in the garden." And then to David, "Do you mind, love? Can you look after … I'm sorry, we weren't introduced."

"Rick, Jack's work colleague. How do you do?"

"Nice to meet you, Rick. Will you talk to David while I go for a walk with Jack?"

Rick nodded and David assured her they'd be fine. "You go and talk to Jack. We'll be okay." He winked at her and said, tongue in cheek, "We'll listen to this music that seems to be Sister Agatha's favourite."

"Cheeky," she whispered and led Jack through the side door into the garden where the summer flowers were in full bloom and the lawns shone in the afternoon sun.

"This garden is always so peaceful," Annie said as the strolled across the lawn. "This is where Bella found her den, the place where she and I hid from the nuns and the rest of the girls in the orphanage."

Jack smiled. "And I bet she was the boss around here," he said confidently. "That was what I fell in love with, her self- assertion. She appeared in the dining room at Pike House like a tornado. My eyes where instantly drawn to her."

"That's Bella alright," Annie agreed. "You know, Jack, I really would like to thank you for loving Bella..." she paused poignantly, "... warts an'all!"

"No need to thank me," Jack stated. "It was easy..." His voice faltered. "It was my fault, Annie. I might as well have put a gun to her head. It would have had the same outcome." Tears streamed down his face and he was overcome with grief.

Annie took his hand and spoke softly. "It was an accident, Jack, a road accident." Her heart went out to the distraught young man and she wept with him.

After a few minutes, they sat in Bella's den and helped each other in their grief by listening and talking things through. "I have to believe Bella is in a happier place," Annie told him. "If we learned one lesson from our Catholic upbringing, it is that the soul is immortal and lives on in Paradise. I find comfort in that. Maybe you will too."

Jack looked wistful. "At this moment in time, I wish I had as much faith as you, but I struggle with the whole religious thing. I sincerely hope Bella is happy, because she was so sad." He dissolved into tears again. "She was so sad when she left me. I was angry and she had told me she was unsure about marrying the first boyfriend she'd had, even though she loved me."

Annie was confused. "We talked about how she felt about you, Jack, and she told me she loved you with all her heart. She was ready to accept your proposal. She never mentioned any of that other stuff to me. She had wondered if love was enough and she was unsure if she would know how to be a good wife."

"That was part of it, but when she saw where I lived, she became all defensive and was overwhelmed by her past," Jack explained. "I believed we had sorted all that stuff out and I truly thought by gently guiding her into my world, bit by bit, she would be ready to take the next step in seeing where I lived and meeting my parents.”

“Do you honestly think Bella needed all that?” Annie asked. “All this is beyond my experience. David and I both live in Half Way House and although we aren’t thinking of marriage, I firmly believe that if we were, we would make the transition together.”

Jack leaned back against the wide tree trunk that formed the back of the den and sighed deeply. “I don’t know now, Annie,” he admitted. “She had a terrible hang-up about having nothing and she often said she had resigned herself to the fact that was what everybody expected of her. I wanted her to look forward and aim high.”

“To dream?” Annie asked softly.

“Exactly,” Jack agreed, “and I thought she was coming round to realising that life is what you make it. She was doing well at work and I know she had been saving her wages. She was very proud of her bank account.”

Annie smiled. “She always told me that dreamers lived in a fantasy world and she didn’t want to hear about dreams and ambitions, but seriously, after she met you, she was coming round to understanding what magic moments in our lives are all about.”

“I guess she was just confused when it came to making one of the biggest decisions of her life,” Jack conjectured. He slapped his hand on his thigh. “And I got angry instead of understanding what she was saying. How could I have been so stupid? How could I be such a fool? What a bloody idiot I am!”

Annie saw how much he was tormenting himself. “Jack,” she said gently. “None of us knows what lies in store for us. Fate is fickle. Bella enriched both our lives and maybe that was what she was meant to do. Her life came to an end in the most tragic way, but we must allow her to rest in peace knowing that we are grateful she was part of our lives even for a short time.”

Jack took Annie’s hand and squeezed it. “How did you get to be so philosophical, Annie? You aren’t old enough to have all that understanding in your pretty little head.”

"If you'd seen me a week ago, you wouldn't believe I was capable of one rational thought and I have no idea where all that came from except that it came from my heart," she told him. "I just know that Bella wouldn't want us to be unhappy, especially when she had found happiness herself for the comparatively short time she had with you. Find your comfort in that, Jack, and I think you'll be fine."

"Thanks, Annie. Thank you very much," Jack said sincerely. "It will take me a long time to get over Bella. At the moment, I still think she'll come flying round the dining room with a tray full of entrées. I will try to move on, but not right now. Thank you again."

"Neither of us will ever forget her. If I have helped you in some small way, it's my pleasure and you're welcome," Annie replied. "And now we should get back to David and Rick. They'll think we've got lost."

Ten

The summer holidays went by slowly and Annie spent several days each week working at Woolworths to earn as much as she might before leaving Half Way House and moving into the nurses' quarters at the General Hospital. David had secured a holiday job at Walker's Tannery. They had managed to continue their relationship and enjoyed each other's company whenever they were able. They spent a lot of their time walking around The Jumbles Country Park and they climbed Rivington Pike as often as they could. By the end of the holidays, they looked fit and healthy, ready to face the next big challenges in their young lives. Bella was never far from Annie's thoughts and she found that as time went by, she was able to talk about her without being upset.

"You know," Annie said as they sat in Rivington Barn having a soft drink after their walk, "I can put down all my strength and confidence to Bella Jones. I wish I could tell her how much I appreciate what she did for me."

David took her hand. "She'll know."

"I believe that too," she said, smiling as she remembered the good times, and becoming more pensive on remembering their differences. "But I knew we would go our separate ways because we were so different. That's a simple fact of life: we meet and we part whatever the circumstances. I'm glad I can feel happy in remembering her."

"Let's hope we'll be happy tomorrow when our results are out," David reminded her.

"What will be, will be," Annie said pragmatically and shrugged. "I'm in the hands of the gods when it comes to that last paper. I hope Bella was urging me on."

Remarkably, Annie and David passed their exams with flying colours. Their relationship had carried them through the trying times and the future looked rosy for them both. When David appeared at breakfast a few mornings later carrying a long white envelope, Annie knew it would be the letter telling him where he had gained a place at university. "Open it," she urged. "What are you waiting for?"

"I'm nervous," he said.

"Why?" Annie asked. "You said you didn't mind where you went so long as you got a place away from Bolton."

David looked down at the envelope in his hand and carefully opened it with his butter knife. The letter was folded to reveal the letterhead – *University of Exeter* – David smiled as he read silently and then, "I've been offered a place at Exeter to read English and Drama with a year of overseas study. Yay!" he whooped, "That's awesome!"

Annie stood up from the table and went to give him a hug. "I'm so pleased for you. Congratulations and well done, you."

"I'm very happy with a place at Exeter. I had already resigned myself to the fact that I wouldn't get an Oxbridge place. An abandoned child who lives in a community home—albeit a very luxurious community home—doesn't quite fit into the Oxbridge ilk," he commented.

"Are you sad about that?" Annie asked.

"Well, more philosophical, I think," David answered. "I always knew I was aiming high when I applied, but I had to try."

"Well, I think it's their loss," Annie told him, "but I'll be sad that you'll be going so far away from me. We'll survive though, won't we?"

"Of course we'll survive,' David said. "We made it this far, didn't we?"

At the end of August, nineteen sixty-one, both Annie and David packed up their belongings and left Half Way House. Annie went to Trinity Street Station to see him off. They cuddled on the platform until his train arrived and hastily kissed before he loaded his suitcase onto the train. "Take care, Annie. I'll write to you when I get settled."

"You take care too and enjoy your course. I'll be thinking of you."

David grinned. "Don't let me interfere with your nursing and your studies. Three years will be up before we know it. Bye, Annie. Love you."

"Love you too, brainbox!" Annie called as the train pulled out of the station and she stood on the platform waving until it went out of sight.

~ * ~

Moving into the nurses' home was easy. Annie marvelled at the way she didn't have to adjust to living in a house of multiple occupancy when some of the other nursing recruits had difficulty settling in. The first few days were spent receiving uniforms, text books, timetables and rosters. Annie knew that her days would be full and she was looking forward to beginning her nursing training. The new uniforms were comfortable and purpose-designed. The dresses were open-necked and the caps were small and inconspicuous on the back of the head. Annie wore the obligatory fob watch pinned to her apron. It was a gift from Sister Augustina who had inspired her to follow her dreams. Annie felt that she belonged in the hospital environment and settled well. The first few weeks passed quickly and with every new day came new challenges, new information, new treatments, new strategies. Only when she went to bed at night did she think of David. She hadn't heard from him in five weeks, but dismissed it as being the settling in process which had prevented him from writing to her.

Eleven

"Hello, Nurse O'Shea," he said as he looked at the name on her badge.

"Hello," Annie replied and looked puzzled at the man in a white coat standing in front of her in the refectory queue.

"With a name like that, you ought to have an Irish accent, to be sure," he quipped.

"I'm not from Ireland," she told him.

"Are you a student nurse?" he asked unnecessarily since she was wearing what all student nurses wore.

She cocked her head to one side and asked bluntly, "Is there something I can help you with?"

Her new friend and colleague, Shirley Strachan, nudged her deliberately. "He's chatting you up, Annie," and she winked at the young man who continued to ask questions. "I'm Shirley," she said coyly.

The young man nodded. "Oh, Annie is it?" he said, delighted that he hadn't had to ask her to find out.

"Anne Marie, actually. Only my friends call me Annie," she stated firmly and with unusual confidence upon meeting a stranger.

The young man spoke confidently. "Well, I shall just have to make sure I'm your friend then. Do you mind if I join you for lunch?"

Annie looked at Shirley, who nodded enthusiastically.

"I'll take that as a yes then," he said and smiled. "Nice to meet you, Anne Marie O'Shea, and your friend, Shirley Strachan. It's like the gathering of the clans, the O'Sheas, the Strachans and the Joneses."

Annie gasped involuntarily and her expression changed from self-assurance to sad bewilderment. She looked down to hide her confusion.

"Have I said something to offend you?" their new acquaintance asked.

Taking a deep breath, Annie managed to say, "No, not at all. I was just caught off guard for a moment. Sorry."

They got their lunches and found a table by the window overlooking the garden. As the young man pulled out their chairs for them, he introduced himself. "I'm Rob Jones...actually Roberto Antonio Jones...Italian mother and Welsh father. I'm a third year physiotherapist here at the General. Sorry if I came on to you too brazenly. I'm often told I should slow down a bit. Not everybody likes an over-confident buffoon who doesn't know when to shut up. Sorry if I offended you."

"You didn't offend *me*," Shirley told him boldly. "It'd take more than an Italian Welshman to upset me." She grinned at Rob. "Nice to meet you," she simpered.

Rob directed his attention to Annie. "Well, Nurse O'Shea, you are very quiet. Are you sure I didn't offend you?"

"I'm sure," she confirmed. "I'm not used to being approached by young men in dinner queues." She laughed a little, thinking, *I'm not used to being approached by men full stop. But he's nice so stop putting barriers up, Annie. Show your more sociable side.* "These first few weeks have been full on. Enjoyable, but really demanding."

"I know the feeling, but we are embarking on very worthwhile careers," he said. "Maybe we can look forward to our time off and relax a little."

"Oh, I'm all for that!" Shirley blurted and nudged Annie again.

"Maybe," Annie considered, "if we have the energy."

Hard work, long hours and very little time for relaxation seemed to be the order of the following months. David was conspicuous by his absence and Annie stopped looking in her mailbox for news from Exeter. In her quiet moments, she wondered why he hadn't written to her as he promised. She couldn't write to him because he hadn't let her know his address when he found his accommodation. Rightly or wrongly, he hadn't secured a place to live before he left Half Way House. When the end of the first year loomed, Annie resigned herself to the fact that it was a case of out of sight, out of mind, and her first love was lost to her forever.

~ * ~

The nursing recruits had two weeks off at the end of August. Annie had confided in Shirley that her boyfriend had gone away to university and not contacted her since. "I have no idea what could have happened, but I know he'll be doing what he always wanted…to get away from Bolton and everything to do with it."

"Maybe that's it then," Shirley said bluntly. "You are obviously a part of Bolton he wanted to leave behind. Perhaps you hold too many bad reminders for him."

"I don't think I'd be a bad memory, Shirl," Annie said defiantly. "We did love each other, but I can't even be sure about that anymore. I thought absence was supposed to make the heart grow fonder, but it seems I have to tell myself it's better to have loved and lost than never to have loved at all. As an English student, he would probably tell me it is too clichéd, but it sums up exactly how I feel."

"Oh come on, Annie, chin up!" Shirley said encouragingly. "I've been out with a few guys and none of them were up to much. They only wanted one thing and I was never prepared to drop my drawers for any of them." She laughed, acknowledging her frank admission. "I decided I would only go out with a boy on my terms. If I didn't want to get involved, I just had one date and called it quits. I think I'd know if I fell in love and then I would do everything within my power to make him happy. Up to now, it hasn't happened."

Annie smiled. "Okay, Shirl. I'll try and adopt that attitude if anybody asks me out. I don't know a lot about men, but I'm a quick learner."

"Let's go to Llandudno for a week when we're on holiday," Shirley suggested. "It will be good to let our hair down and get some sea air in our lungs. Shall I book us a hotel on the promenade?"

"Will I like Llandudno?" Annie asked. "I've never been on holiday before, but I think I like the sound of it. Do what you have to do, Shirl, and let me know how much."

"Great! I'll get onto it this afternoon," Shirley said with conviction. "Llandudno, here we come!

~ * ~

On Saturday, the day after they finished work, they packed their cases and went on a coach to Llandudno, North Wales. The journey seemed to take ages, but Annie didn't mind. She was seeing places she had only ever imagined and when the marble church at Bodelwyddan appeared, she marvelled at its tall white spire. St Asaph was a stopping place and several people got off the coach to begin their holiday. When the coach stopped again at Rhyl and Colwyn Bay, Annie thought they would never reach their destination. "How much longer, Shirl?" she asked like an eager child.

"Fifteen minutes or so," Shirley replied as the driver pulled out of Colwyn Bay and took the coast road towards Rhos-on-Sea and Penrhyn Bay.

Climbing the hill out of Penrhyn Bay, they reached a bend in the road around Little Ormes Head which revealed Conwy Bay and Llandudno in all its Victorian splendour. Annie was enthralled. "Would you look at that now?" she cried. "I have never seen anything like it."

"I knew you'd like it, Annie," Shirley told her. "We'll climb the Little Orme and we'll go on the little tram to the top of the Great Orme. We are going to have so much fun." Then to the driver, "Will you drop us off at the St Tudno Hotel near the pier, please driver?"

The driver slowed down on North Parade. "I'll drop you here," he said. "But you'll have to go the Mostyn Broadway Coach Station when you are going back to Bolton."

"Okay, thanks," Shirley said. "Come on, Annie. We're here!"

Once checked into their accommodation, the two girls changed into shorts and tee shirts and made their way down to the beach. Annie removed her sandals as soon as she set foot on the sand. "I'm so happy, Shirl," she cried as she took her friend's hand and pulled her towards the sea, on its way in for high tide. "Come on! I'm going to dip my toes in the sea!"

"It'll be freezing, girl. Just warning you," Shirley advised.

"Ahhhh, it's freezing!" Annie shrieked.

"What did I just tell you, you ninny, and you've no towel to dry your feet. The sand will stick to your toes and your sandals will rub blisters on your heels!" Shirley was laughing at Annie's behaviour and Annie joined in laughing at her own recklessness.

"Oh jiddy 'eck," she complained. "Why didn't you tell me before?"

Half an hour later, they were walking to the end of the pier where they bought ice- creams and leisurely strolled back to the hotel to change for dinner.

The weather treated them kindly for the first few days and they spent their days on the beach, sunbathing, swimming in the still chilly sea, talking to nearby holidaymakers and generally having the most relaxing time. When the clouds made the days dull, they wandered along Mostyn Street, shop window gazing and sometimes buying souvenirs to take home and remind them of their trip.

By Thursday they had climbed the Little Orme as planned and taken the tram up to the top of the Great Orme. Across the road from the tram station, they found the best fish and chip shop in the world and had lunch there on a couple of occasions. On Thursday night, after going to Conwy Castle and visiting the smallest house in Wales, they decided they would have a night out on the town. They discovered a pub with live music at the top end of Mostyn Street and decided to give it a try.

"I've never been in a pub, Shirl," Annie admitted. "What will I drink?"

Shirley, wide-eyed, exclaimed, "You've never been in a pub? Blood and stomach pills, Annie. I went in a pub when I was sixteen. I didn't think there was a girl in Bolton who hadn't been in a pub by the time they were eighteen and legally allowed to drink. Where have you been all your life?"

Annie felt uncomfortable. "Where I was brought up, we didn't have such liberties, Shirl. I'm an orphan, don't forget and... well, we just didn't go out at night."

"Aw, you poor thing," Shirley said sympathetically. "Well, all that was then and now is now, so you have time to make up for all you missed out on before you reach twenty-one. I'll look after you and show you the ropes."

The pub was full of young people and the live band played all the popular stuff that Annie had seen and heard on television. Six-Five Special and Juke Box Jury had introduced her to pop music and she had learned a long time ago that girls fell in love with Elvis Presley, but she thought she would rather fall in love with Cliff Richard. Hearing the music live was a new experience for her.

"I love this!" she shouted at Shirley. "Mind you, I think I'll be deaf by the end of the evening."

"What?" Shirley shouted back and they both dissolved into laughter as they drank their shandies.

Surrounded by singing and dancing young people, the girls edged their way to a corner where they might see the stage clearly and renew their drinks easily at the bar.

"Can I buy you a drink?" the guy asked Shirley.

Shirley beamed at him. "Only if you buy my friend one as well," she said with a glint in her eye.

"My mate will buy her one," he replied and he beckoned his mate to join them. "What will it be?"

Shirley thought for a moment. "I think we'll have Pimm's number one seeing as you're paying," she said cheekily. "Number one has gin in it, doesn't it?"

"Saucy little madam, aren't you?" he said. "I'm Brian, by the way."

"Hello Brian-by-the-way," Shirley continued in her own inimitable style. "I'm Shirley and this is Annie."

Brian's mate had sidled up to them. "I'm Gareth."

Annie nodded and sipped her Pimm's, wrinkling her nose as she did so. Gareth, on seeing Annie's reaction to the drink, nudged her arm and said pointedly, "You'd better drink that, darlin'. It cost a fortune."

Brian was already taking Shirley in a clinch and was nuzzling her neck. Shirley giggled and Annie was taken aback. Gareth, taking Brian's lead, put his arm around Annie and pulled her towards him. Trying to pull away, Annie struggled to stop him from kissing her and in the process spilled her drink down his shirt.

"You clumsy bi..." he shouted just as two strong arms pulled him away from Annie and marched him towards the door where the bouncer took over and threw Gareth out of the bar.

Annie stood there dumbfounded, holding her handbag to her chest until her knight in shining armour returned. "What are you doing here?" she exclaimed.

"I'm doing the same as you, I think, listening to live music. Good, aren't they?"

"Yes they are, but it's deafening. I think I'll just go outside for a breather." She tapped on Shirley's shoulder and signalled that she was going outside. Shirley put up a thumb behind Brian's back and continued with her snogging in full view of everybody.

Once outside, Annie turned to her escort and said, "Thanks, Rob. I don't know what I would have done without you."

"I couldn't stand by and let my favourite student nurse be manhandled by a less than gallant Welshman," Rob told her.

Annie smiled at him. "Thank you, but I asked you before, what are you doing here? You didn't follow Shirley and me to Llandudno, did you?"

Rob laughed. "I don't think so. My parents live here and own a restaurant in Craig-y-Don, just after Bodafon Farm fields and almost opposite the paddling pool. Have you been up there?"

"We went up there to climb the Little Orme, but I didn't notice a restaurant," Annie told him. "We have had such a brilliant time. I love Llandudno and I had no idea you lived here."

"I don't, but I come here every time I have a couple of days off. It's a good place to unwind."

Annie shivered in the cold night air blowing in from the sea. Rob removed his jacket and slipped it round her shoulders. "Let's go for a walk along the prom," he suggested.

"But what about Shirley? She won't know where we are," Annie said, concerned that her friend would be worried about her.

"She won't even know we're missing," Rob assured her. "You probably won't see her until daylight tomorrow morning. She sure seemed to be having a good time as we left."

They walked along Trevor Street to the promenade and across the road towards the pier. "I love the pier," Annie said. "We have made it our daily exercise to walk to the end of it and back. We haven't done it at night though, but look at all the lights reflected in the sea. I love lights. No matter where you are, they give a sense of never being alone..."

"Lights are beautiful," he agreed, "and they are certainly a sign of life when you are lost on Mount Snowdon."

"Have you been lost up there? Shirley and I were planning to go up on the mountain train tomorrow and then maybe walk back down if the weather is fine," she told him. "Can you really get lost up there?"

"Not in broad daylight, so long as you keep to the paths," he explained. "My mates and I, when we were brash little schoolboys, went climbing up there one time and one of them broke his ankle. It was dark by the time the mountain rescue team found us. And..." he paused preparing himself for his big announcement. "... my light—my torchlight—guided them to us."

"Wonderful!" Annie laughed.

When they arrived at the end of the pier, all was quiet and still. The breeze had abated and all that could be heard was the gentle lapping of the waves against the supporting pillars below. Lights atop of the Great Orme twinkled to their left and far away to the right and out to sea as the coastline veered left, were the lights of Colwyn Bay and Rhyl. Annie was enthralled and automatically she took Rob's arm and squeezed it affectionately. "I feel so relaxed and happy," she whispered. "I have often dreamed of places like this, but to be here and take it all in, just overwhelms me."

"You are so sweet, Annie O'Shea. You seem to appreciate the important things in life, not like most young people today who just want cash and record players and fashionable clothes and everything else that costs a lot of money. Somehow, you have an effortless charm and I like that."

"I'm not sure I understand what you're saying, but thank you. I do my best."

Rob gave her a hug, holding her close for a little longer than a hug should allow. Annie could feel his warm breath on her cheek. She looked up at him and his lips met hers, gentle and loving, respectful, yet intimate.

Afterwards, they walked hand in hand back to the hotel, talking of future plans and ambitions. "Have you always lived in Bolton, Annie?" Rob asked.

"I have," she replied and wondered how much she should tell him. "I was brought up by nuns in an orphanage." She waited for his response.

"Oh wow!" he said, compassion in his tone. "Should I say I'm sorry, or just accept it without question?"

"However you like," she answered. "It wasn't what you would consider a normal upbringing, but I survived and with the help of a very kind lady in the community home where I lived from being sixteen, I completed my A levels and was accepted on the nursing course."

"If it isn't a rude question, how old are you now?" he asked, not bluntly, more with genuine interest.

"I'll be twenty in September, I think."

Rob slowed his pace and looked at Annie, curiosity written all over his face. "You think?"

Annie smiled. "The nuns gave us a birthday in the absence of a birth certificate. I was left there when I was two, sometime in the month of June, nineteen forty-four...a note pinned to my coat said I was two. Apparently, a doctor decided that from my physical development, I was probably approaching my third birthday, so the nuns assigned the fourteenth of September to me."

Rob was very quiet and listened as Annie told him a little about Bella. "She was a live-wire, but with a heart of gold. It is so sad that she will never see the world as the free spirit she embodied. I miss her all the time, but it does get easier with each passing day."

When they reached the gates of the pier, they wandered a few yards up the prom and sat in one of the Victorian wrought iron shelters facing the sea.

"That's the saddest story I have ever heard," Rob said quietly. "How do you continue with your own life having experienced such tragedy?"

Annie smiled. "You remember all the good things, and for me, I can never forget how hard she worked in making me stand up for myself. If I am strong in character, it's totally down to Bella Jones."

"That's interesting," Rob said. "Same surname as mine. Mind you, I can't even hazard a guess how many Joneses there are in Wales. Did the nuns assign her name to her too, or ..."

"I guess that was her name when she arrived at St Anthony's," Annie explained. "She probably had a name label like I had pinned to my coat. I do know that she was a newborn baby when she was handed in."

Rob placed his arm around Annie and she rested her head on his shoulder. They sat in silence, listening to the waves as they lapped the pebbles on the beach. He lifted her chin with a soft, gentle hand and kissed her again, this time holding her close and feeling her beating heart next to his.

"Time to go," he said looking at his watch. "It's almost midnight and we don't want your landlady locking you out."

"I have a key in my handbag, but if Shirley isn't there when we get back, I think she might be throwing pebbles at my window to let her in," she informed him.

They reached the hotel and Shirley was standing on the step waiting for them. "Oh, I see," she said haughtily. "I turn my back for two minutes and you take up with any Tom, Dick or Harry."

"Excuse me, Nurse Strachan, I'm not any Tom, Dick, or Harry," Rob informed her with the same haughtiness Shirley had displayed. "I'm a respectable local looking after your friend while you were busy making out with a complete stranger!"

"Touché, Rob," she said. "I concede defeat. Where's the key, Annie? I'm flippin' freezing here."

Annie rummaged in her bag for the key and handed it to Shirley. "Have you been here long?" she asked.

"No, not really," Shirley admitted. "That Brian had arms like an octopus, but at least he kept me warm until his taxi came to take him back to...wait a minute... I need to remember how to say it... back to Penmamore."

"Penmaenmawr," Rob corrected.

"What you said," Shirley quipped, pointing a finger at Rob. "He said he'd like to go up Snowdon with us tomorrow. Do you mind, Annie?"

"So long as he doesn't bring his friend with him, I'll be fine," Annie told her.

"Oh, he won't do that," Shirley assured her. "He offered, but I said if he brought that Gareth, he can forget about me."

Rob stood by and listened to what Shirley was saying and turning to Annie, he asked, "Do you mind if I come with you, Annie? I promise I won't let you lose your way."

Annie laughed. "That would be good," she said. "See you here at ten o'clock."

Rob went on his way and the girls went in the hotel and up to their room.

As they lay in bed, Shirley related her evening with Brian. "He's a bit of a fast cat, Annie, but he's a good kisser."

Annie laughed. "Describe a good kisser, Shirl. How do you distinguish between a good kisser and a bad?"

"Well, you know, when you get butterflies in your stomach and you want to kiss him back."

"Oh, I see," Annie said with a longing in her voice. "I see."

Shirley sighed and turned over in her bed. "What about you and Rob then?" she asked sleepily.

"Yeah," Annie replied. "He's nice." And they both drifted off to sleep.

The following morning, Rob turned up in his car. "It'll be easier than waiting for a bus to take you to Snowdonia. We might as well have the comfort of door to door, so to speak."

"That's great," Annie told him. "Thanks, Rob."

Shirley and Brian sat in the back seat and were smooching most of the way to Llanberis where they took the mountain train to the summit of Mount Snowdon. The sun was shining as the little train pulled away from the station. As they approached the summit, the clouds appeared and they found themselves chugging through cold, misty air. The temperature dropped drastically and as they jumped down from the train, it hit them. "It's a good job we brought our sweaters," Shirley announced, dancing around to keep warm. "We'd have ended up like abominable snowmen otherwise."

They all laughed and climbed the final few feet up to the peak. "On a clear day, you can see Northern Ireland, England and Scotland from up here," Rob told them. "It's a pity about this low cloud."

"I'm still glad we came, though," Annie said. "I can cross it off my bucket list...the one that doesn't exist at the moment."

"It's a good place to start, though," Rob agreed. "Shall we have a coffee in the café before we start our trek down?"

~ * ~

The day after their trip to Snowdonia, it was time for the girls to leave. They packed their cases and walked to the bus station on Mostyn Broadway. When they arrived at the bay where the coach was standing, Rob was waiting for them.

"Hello," Annie greeted him. "What are you doing here?"

"That's the second time you've asked that in the last two days," he informed her.

"True, but what *are* you doing here?" she asked again with a smile.

"I wondered if you would like a lift back to Bolton," he explained. "It will be more comfortable and I won't go all around the houses like the coach will on its route."

"But we've got return tickets," Shirley said.

"That's okay. Just tell the driver you won't be taking your seats. He'll understand," Rob advised.

"Sounds good to me," Shirley said, "but you'll have to drop me off in Westhoughton. I'm staying with my parents for a few days before I start back at work."

"Not a problem, Shirl," Rob told her as he loaded their cases in the boot. "Annie, you sit in the front with me. Shirley can have the back seat all to herself."

Twelve

After dropping Shirley off at her parents' house in Westhoughton, Rob turned to Annie and said, "Where next, Nurse O'Shea?"

"I'm going back to the nurses' home at the General," she answered quietly.

Rob noticed her demeanour. "Are you all right, Annie?"

"I'm fine," she said.

"No, you're not," he told her. "I can see something is bothering you. Talk to me."

Annie thought carefully before she spoke. "Shirley asked me to spend a few days at her parents' house. She said I could have her bed and she'd sleep on the sofa in the living room. I told her I couldn't let her do that and she needed time on her own with her parents."

"So what's worrying you?" Rob asked gently.

"The truth is, I lied," she disclosed. "I have never lived in a house with a family. My best friend died because she was afraid of not being able to adapt to a normal life, for want of better terminology. I never understood how she felt until now. I feel totally overwhelmed with having to try to fit in. I hate myself for it, but I can't help it."

Rob took her hand and looked into her eyes. "Dear little Annie," he said. "You can't think like that. What I know of you, I think you'll fit in wherever you go."

"I know I'd give it a good go, but thoughts of Bella and what happened to her, are haunting me at the moment, and the funny thing is, I know she'd absolutely berate me for feeling like this."

"Don't be sad, Annie," he implored. "You are not alone. I'm not too far away in the residential block and whenever you feel lonely, give me a call and I'll come running."

"That's kind of you, but you'll be working next week, won't you?" she reminded him.

"I'll sort something out. Just leave it to me."

When they arrived back at the hospital, Rob kissed her on the cheek and bid her a hasty goodbye. Annie went to her room, unpacked her case and made her way to the laundry to do her washing. Everywhere was quiet. All the student nurses were on holiday, or on home leave. A black cloud of loneliness enveloped Annie and filled her with sadness. She dried her clothes in the tumble dryer, ironed them and took them back to her room to put them away. As she was just about to sit and read the book David had once recommended, Thomas Hardy's *Far From The Madding Crowd*, there was a knock on her door. Startled, she went to open it. "What are you doing here?"

"Not again!" Rob exclaimed. "Can you be ready in the morning for a couple more days away?"

Annie was confused.

"I'll pick you up at..."

"I have to go to Mass in the morning," she told him.

"What time?"

"I think there's an early Mass so I'll go to that," she said.

"Can you be ready for ten o'clock?" Rob asked her excitedly. "I have a surprise for you. I'm taking an extra couple of days of my holiday allowance. Pack some warm clothes and comfortable shoes. We are going to Windermere. I'll explain tomorrow. I have to get back now and cover for Simon Croston. He's going to cover one day for me so I can take you to The Lakes. That way I can keep at least one day of my holidays for later. It's very generous of him at such short notice."

Annie was excited. The trip to the Lake District was completely out of the blue. She was ready and waiting at the door when Rob pulled up in his pale blue Hillman Minx.

"It isn't very often that anybody surprises me," she told him as he opened the door for her and then put her case in the boot. "I know I'll like the Lake District. I have seen pictures of it in the magazines in the common room."

"I know you'll love it," Rob told her as they left Bolton behind and journeyed north along the M6 motorway. "When I left you yesterday, I phoned Mum and Dad to see if their cottage was vacant at the moment. Fortunately, it isn't being rented until the end of the month so we can use it for a few days as long as we leave it clean and tidy when we leave."

"Sounds wonderful," Annie said. "When did I get so lucky?"

Rob shrugged and smiled. "I think you are due a bit of luck, don't you?"

"If you say so," she agreed. "Thank you."

They stopped for a lunch break at Newby Bridge and watched the swans on the lake as they munched on salmon and cucumber sandwiches provided by the hospital catering staff as a favour to Rob.

"You must have very persuasive powers to get chef to make sandwiches for us," Annie commented as she threw the last bit of crust to the swans and ducks on the lake.

"I just worked my magic," he said, feigning conceit.

Annie laughed. "I always knew somebody would bring magic into my life, but I didn't expect it in the form of salmon sandwiches."

Rob laughed with her and instinctively gave her a hug.

Annie took his hand. "You know," she said seriously, "I'm pleased that you are able to show affection so easily. It helps me to accept that physical part of a friendship. A couple of years ago, I would have run a mile if I thought you were going to give me a hug."

"It comes naturally when you are with somebody you like," Rob told her.

"Thanks," she said thinking, *I learned that very quickly when I was with David.*

Annie gasped when they arrived at the cottage. It was picture-postcard pretty with roses round the door. It didn't have a thatched roof, but it was built of Lakeland stone. It was set back from the road and surrounded by woodland, backing onto Lake Windermere. Inside it was warm and cosy with a wood burning stove in the centre of the open-plan living room and kitchen. French windows opened onto a well-tended garden and a path led down to the water's edge where a rowing boat was moored.

"What do you think?" Rob asked tentatively.

"I think it's the stuff dreams are made of," she said as she surveyed the little piece of heaven. "How come you know me so well?"

"Intuition, little Annie. Intuition."

They left their luggage at the foot of the stairs and went out on the lake, Rob rowing masterfully and Annie sitting back and marvelling at the scenery around her. "This is wonderful, Rob. Thank you again for bringing me."

"My pleasure," he said smiling at the beautiful young lady in front of him. "Has anybody ever told you, you look like a blonde, petite version of Audrey Hepburn?"

"I was once told I look like Petula Clark, but actually, I just want to look like me," she told him. "I would hate to think I was trying to be somebody else."

Rob smiled, a smile that displayed genuine appreciation of Annie's unique character. "I reckon the nuns did a great job with you, Annie O'Shea." He steered the boat to the ramp and held her hand as she stepped out. "I'll tie up the boat. You go into the kitchen and see if there's any food in the fridge."

"There's nothing in here except a carton of long-life milk," she called to Rob as he made his way back to the cottage.

"Come on then," he called back. "We'll slip into Ambleside and stock up for the next couple of days. If there's anything left when we decide to leave, we'll take it with us."

After a dinner of sausage and mash with onion gravy, all prepared by Rob, they had fruit and ice cream for dessert and settled down to watch *Sunday Night at The London Palladium* on television as they sipped on glasses of Mateus Rosé.

"I feel as though I won't need to eat for a week," Annie said. "I'm as full as an egg!"

"What do you think of the wine?" Rob asked. "I chose a light one for you to try. Judging by your face in the pub last week, I thought you wouldn't like anything stronger."

"I like this," she said. "I don't think I'll ever be a wine connoisseur, but I could get used to this."

As they sat on the settee and watched television, Rob put his arm around Annie. She snuggled close to him, resting her head on his shoulder. With only the glow from the television screen lighting the room, there was an atmosphere of complete calm; the air warm and comfortable.

"How are you coping with living in a family home?" Rob asked.

Annie sat upright and glared at him. "So that's what you are doing, is it?" she questioned. "I should have realised as soon as we arrived here, but I was too pre-occupied with admiring the cottage. You must think I'm a complete noodle."

"Never!" Rob joked.

Annie gave him a playful nudge. "To be honest, I feel very comfortable with it. The house doesn't faze me like I imagined it would and the company just makes me feel welcome and ..." She stopped abruptly.

"...and what?" Rob asked.

"It doesn't matter," she said dismissively.

"It matters to me," Rob said firmly, but without animosity.

Annie shifted her position, tucked her legs under her until she was kneeling, facing the young man who had taken her under his wing. Her thoughts were confused. *Rob is so kind and helpful. He's like Bella in so many ways...perhaps more subtle, but I can see similar traits in his personality.* She untucked her legs and leaned back on the settee and looked sideways, trying to smile at Rob. *Oh my goodness, his name is Jones too and his mother's Italian...oh my goodness. Don't go there, Annie. Just don't go there.*

At eleven o'clock, Rob turned off the television and said, "Time for bed, I think. I'm planning a big day tomorrow." He kissed Annie goodnight and showed her to her room.

"Goodnight, Rob, and thank you for today. I have really enjoyed it."

"My pleasure," he replied as she went into her room. "Bathroom on the left," he called. "You use it first."

Annie closed the bedroom door quietly and leaned on it, reflecting on what had taken place. *I can't quite believe what is happening,* she thought. She opened her case and took out her nightdress, crisp white cotton with *broderie anglaise* at the hem and a delicate ribbon to tie at the neck. She smiled to herself. *What a difference from the flannelette regulation issue nighties we all wore at St Anthony's. The first thing I bought when we left was a pair of baby doll pyjamas. I adored them!* She went to the bathroom in her nightie and after she removed her make-up and brushed her teeth, she returned to her room. As she lay between crisp cotton sheets, she hugged herself and sighed. *I like Rob and I've kissed him numerous times. Am I being promiscuous? His kisses were warm and affectionate, not at all like David's. His were kind of immature by comparison.* She sat up and rested her chin on her knees. *Dear David. I loved him so much and I believed he loved me, but now that I have met Rob, the feelings I had for David don't seem to matter so much anymore.* She repeated her previous thought. *Am I being promiscuous? Well, according to Shirley who has kissed numerous boys, it's what life is all about. If she doesn't consider it's promiscuous, I won't either.* She snuggled under the eiderdown and went to sleep feeling completely relaxed.

When she woke the following morning, the sun was shining in through her window. She stretched out, arms above her head, the stretch reaching from her finger tips to her toes. She showered quickly and dressed in shorts and tee shirt before she skipped down the stairs to find Rob squeezing orange juice. "That looks good," she commented.

"Good morning," he said enthusiastically without looking up. "Did you sleep well?"

"I did," she replied. "Did you?"

Orange juice ready, he placed the glasses on the kitchen table. "Oh my..." he gasped as he caught sight of Annie bathed in sunlight, her wet hair shining like golden corn and her electric blue eyes sparkling as she smiled. Her expression asked him what was wrong.

"You look lovely, Annie." That was all he could say.

"Well, thank you," she replied and sat at the table to drink her orange juice. "What are we doing today?"

Rob took a deep breath to compose himself. "I thought we would go to Coniston and climb the Old Man," he said. "It'll be very invigorating and will blow the cobwebs away."

Annie laughed. "What is the Old Man?" she asked.

"It's a fell, quite high, but walkable," he explained. "What size shoe are you?"

Annie looked puzzled. "Four, why?"

"We keep a supply of hiking boots in the cottage. Four is standard so I'm sure we'll have some to fit."

"How many other people have worn them?" she asked not hiding her distaste.

"Only my mum, as far as I know. People who rent the cottage usually have their own," he told her. "Don't worry, we'll buy you a pair of thick hiking socks so your feet will be protected from any possible foot mange," he joked.

Annie blushed. "Sorry," she said. "The nuns were so strict on personal hygiene and wearing each other's shoes was a definite no-no. Shoes and underwear were the only things they ever bought new for us."

"You'll be fine, but we can buy you new boots if you prefer, but they'll need to be walked in before you actually go on a hike. Trust me, Annie. You'll be okay in Mum's boots with new socks," Rob told her affably. "Now, cereal or toast or both?"

~ * ~

The fell walk was indeed invigorating and Annie felt fully refreshed. "That was so enjoyable," she said as they changed their shoes ready for a trip to Hawkshead for lunch. "Thanks for bringing me, Rob. I sha..."

"You don't have to keep thanking me, Annie," Rob interrupted. "I just want you to enjoy the break."

"Sorry," she offered.

"And no need to apologise," he added, giving her a friendly hug.

"Sorr... Oops, there I go again, but it's difficult for me not to say thank you when you are lavishing me with all sorts of things and experiences I haven't had before," she explained. "And for me not to apologise if I've said something to offend you goes against the grain. I'll try to get used to it though. Promise."

The day was filled with new places, new experiences and new feelings. Rob was happy making Annie happy and he showed his affection openly by hand-holding, affectionate hugs and the occasional peck on the cheek. When they arrived back at the cottage, they decided to have pizza and a bottle of sparkling wine for dinner. "I'll maka you the besta pizza you've ever tasted," Rob said. "Mamma mia! You'll have the besta Italian experience ofa your life!"

Annie laughed. "It will be another first for me so I'm looking forward to it."

~ * ~

After dinner, they lit a fire to combat the cold evening air. Full of pizza and pleasantly happy with the wine, they snuggled on the settee in front of the log burner, wallowing in the warmth and in each other's company. "Today has been wonderful," Annie said dreamily. "Please accept that as my being grateful without saying the banned words."

Rob laughed and held her close. "Annie?"

"Yes?"

"Can I tell you something?"

"Yes," she repeated, totally distracted by the flames dancing inside the stove.

"I think I'm falling in love with you," he whispered.

Annie sat bolt upright. She stared at Rob with wide questioning eyes. "Don't do that!" she cried.

"Do what?" he asked confused by her reaction.

"Fall in love with me."

"But why not?" he questioned. "This isn't another orphan thing that gets in the way of forming relationships, is it?"

"No," she told him. "The last person who told me he loved me walked out of my life a year ago and forgot all about me. I have had neither sight nor sound from him since. I don't want to risk that with you."

"There is no risk involved, Annie," he assured her. "I'm here with you, I work in the same place and I have rooms next door to the nurses' quarters."

Annie sighed deeply. "Would it work when we are with each other twenty-four-seven?" Her thoughts were running away with her again. *This is what Bella was worried about. But I'm not Bella, I'm me. What if David comes back to find me? But I don't think I love him anymore. Rob is nice, more than nice- and I do like him; I like him a lot. Don't be silly, Annie, and go with the flow as Margot told you.* She smiled, cupped Rob's handsome face in her hands and kissed him softly, gently, fervently. Rob responded and felt her heart racing as he drew her close.

"Oh, Annie," he whispered. "I love you; I want you; I..."

"Make love to me," she whispered. "Please make love to me."

He took her in his arms and carried her upstairs to his room. He placed her on the bed and slowly removed her clothes and his own. Breathing deeply and fast, he whispered, "Are you sure about this, darling Annie?"

She nodded without speaking.

Afterwards as they lay in each other's arms, she closed her eyes and thought of Bella. *Bella was so right. I did float on a cloud somewhere outside my body and yet the feeling of loving satisfaction was deep inside my soul.* She opened her eyes and found Rob looking at her lovingly. "I love you," she said with sincerity.

"I love you too," he replied. "Will you sleep in here with me tonight?"

"I will," she said sleepily. "Goodnight, Rob. Sweet dreams."

Thirteen

The holidays were over and they were back at work. Annie only saw Rob in her lunch breaks on the days she was rostered on day shifts. Rob's work only involved day shifts so he spent his evenings alone when Annie worked nights. Occasionally, he sneaked her into his rooms when time allowed. Annie was still a student and one day a week, she had to go to college to do the theory part of the course. She qualified as a State Registered Nurse (SRN) in nineteen sixty-four.

Shirley had left the profession as she and Brian had a baby and got married in that order. Annie immersed herself in her work and spent time with Rob on her days off. She saved as much as she was able to put down a deposit on a house and when she felt she was ready to go house hunting, she told Rob on the day they went to the Smithills Coaching House for lunch.

Rob was confused. "Why can't we buy a house together?" he asked.

Annie looked at the man she loved and tried to find words that would make him understand her feelings. "Can I ask you to try to understand what I am going to say?" she requested. "I am twenty-two years old and..."

"Please, Annie, not the orphan thing again," he implored.

"Not really, but it may have something to do with that, just a little bit." Her voice faltered as she spoke. "I'm really not expecting you to understand completely, but I have this desperate need to have a home that is totally mine. I would like you to be able to stay with me whenever you like, but I want to make a home whole-heartedly for myself. I have dreamed about it for ever and it is important to me to call it my home...*my* home."

"But it would still be your home if we bought it together, wouldn't it?" Rob argued.

"I understand what you're saying, but humour me, Rob. I need to fulfil a life-long ambition to own a home by myself. I need to feel it is mine and I wouldn't be able to do that if it were half yours."

Rob was becoming agitated. "That's the most selfish thing I have ever heard coming from your lips, Annie," he said bluntly. "Please don't make this into our first row. Why can't we start a new home together?"

Annie sighed and felt tears rising in her eyes. "I knew you wouldn't understand, but when I lay in my rickety bed in the orphanage, I promised myself that one day I would possess my own home. I have to do it and I hope you'll still be there with me."

"Don't turn on the tears, Annie," he said with a harshness Annie had never heard before. "I do understand, I do, but isn't it time you turned your back on your past and accepted what your life is all about now? God knows I've done my best to show you that life after the orphanage is much better than what you have experienced before. My parents have accepted you and you've managed to get along with them in their home without talking about St Anthony's, or the nuns, or Bella. I thought we had solved the problems together. When you told them you were an orphan, they didn't say a word. In fact, they have never mentioned it since, so can't you see it didn't matter to them?"

Annie sniffed and wiped away her tears with her napkin. Her memory was telling her a different story. *I'd like to remind him it was as though I'd dropped a bombshell when I told them. They went silent...only for a few moments, but it was obvious they were affected by what I had said. That in itself was enough to tell me they were unsure about how they should react.* "I'm grateful for everything you have done for me, Rob, but my background has moulded who I am and I can never forget it. I won't forget it just because I am in a much stronger position in life now."

"I'm not asking you to forget it, but I don't want you to let it influence how you organise your life from now on," Rob told her firmly. "You are a much stronger person than you were a few years ago. I'm not sure I like what's happening here."

"Will you think about it then, Rob?" she asked, aware of her own stubbornness and wondering where it would take her.

"I will," he agreed, "but I can't really comprehend your sudden inflexible attitude. Please don't let it affect our relationship."

"It won't," she said.

~ * ~

Three months later, Annie had bought her house, a Victorian terrace, on Stanley Lane, just a ten minute walk from the hospital. Rob had failed to persuade her to allow him to buy with her and he struggled to be interested. "I wish you'd be happy for me," she said as he helped carry the last piece of furniture into the house.

"I am happy for you, Annie, but I'd be happier if you'd let me be a part of all this with you," he answered. "I still don't understand why you have dug in your heels like you have."

"Will you stay for our first night in my house?" she asked.

"I don't think so," he replied. "You can enjoy *your* house on your own. I'm sure you will wallow in your ownership alone instead of sharing it with me."

Annie stared at him. "Oh my goodness," she declared. "Say it how it is, won't you? I knew you weren't happy that I bought the house without you, but I thought you could live with it. Where does this leave us then, Rob?"

"Wherever you want it to, Annie," he said, his tone indifferent. "I thought I had found the girl of my dreams; I know I had, but all this has left me completely baffled. You said this wouldn't interfere with our relationship, but it has. I'll always be there for you, but I'm not sure anymore that our future is together. The sooner you rid yourself of the demons of the past, the better you will face the future."

"I think I have rid myself of those demons," she told him, "but I will never forget where I came from, not for you; not for anybody."

"I'm sorry you feel like that," Rob said sadly. "If we stay together, I don't think I could live with the constant reminders, Annie. You'll never be truly happy if you allow yourself to be haunted by ghosts of the past. Believe me, dwelling on the past is not in your best interest. I'll be off now. See you at work tomorrow."

The first night in her new home was not how she had planned. Instead of snuggling up to Rob in her king size bed, she wrapped herself in the duvet and wept into her pillow. *Dear God,* she prayed silently. *Please guide me to where I am supposed to be. Give me the good grace to acknowledge my past and view what comes next with a mind open to change. Bless Rob when he begins his search for his soulmate. I see now that it isn't me. Please give him somebody else who appreciates all that he is and all that he will be. Amen.*

~ * ~

Annie was happy in her work. Four years passed and by the time she was twenty-six, she had been promoted to Nursing Sister and was working on the maternity ward. She started her midwifery training and loved her new focus. Rob had moved back to live with his parents in Llandudno and was working in Glan Clwyd Hospital in Denbighshire. He had said goodbye to Annie, but had occasionally kept in touch with her by letter ... *The arrangement with my parents is temporary. I am looking to buy a flat in St Asaph, the place where you admired the marble church. I'm enjoying my job and I'm meeting new people...*

Annie smiled and thought, *Maybe that's his way of telling me he has met someone else to share his life, but that's fine. I don't begrudge him some happiness. I obviously couldn't give him what he wanted in a wife. He never mentioned marriage to me which, in hindsight, was a bit odd seeing we had been together for three years and we were so in love. At the time, it didn't enter my head. Maybe I subconsciously felt it was never to be.*

She picked up an *Evening News* on her way to work one Saturday evening in November nineteen sixty-nine. She intended to read it during her break, so she placed it in her locker for later. Two of her ladies were in the early stages of labour and earlier in the day, one had progressed more rapidly than anticipated. As soon as Annie arrived on the ward, her lady was being wheeled into the delivery room. Within minutes the new mother was pushing out the little life from within her and Annie, as always, was overjoyed in helping to bring a new life into the world. By the end of her shift, she realised she hadn't had a break all night and she forgot about her newspaper until several days later when she retrieved it from under several experimental plastic aprons that were being worn with a view to replacing the conventional cotton ones. "Oh heck," she said to the nurse cadet assisting her, "I intended reading this last Saturday. Ah well, old news, but it will keep me occupied while I have a cup of tea. Just check Mrs Slater in bed three, will you, Jean? She won't be ready for a while, but she might need reassuring. She's very nervous."

Annie made her tea, had a couple of biscuits from the communal biscuit barrel and took her newspaper from her locker. The front page was full of pros and cons of capital punishment. Parliament had voted to abolish hanging and still the papers were full of the rights and wrongs of the death penalty. Inside, on the second page, was a big headline, *AUSTRALIA BECKONS.* "Looks interesting," she said to herself and read the article in silence. *The Australian Government will be continuing the migration scheme for only two more years. British subjects are still able to migrate to Australia for the sum of £10 per person. Conditions of the scheme remain the same – stay for two years or refund the balance of the fare which is around £110. Australia is a comparatively new country and offers wonderful opportunities for all. Contact the Australian Embassy for details.*

Annie took her paper home after her shift and left it open on her kitchen table so she might read it again later. The paper was there for days and she read the article several times. *I'll look into it during my holidays at Christmas. I'll go to Manchester after the new year and see what I can find out,* she thought. *Maybe that's the new challenge I need.*

One Sunday morning early in the new year, out of the blue, her telephone rang. "Hello, Annie O'Shea here."

"Annie, it's me, Rob."

"My goodness, to what do I owe this pleasure? It's good to hear you," she said without sounding too enthusiastic.

"I have to talk to you," Rob said more seriously now. "I..."

She heard panic in his voice. "Slow down, Rob," she told him. "You'll give yourself a heart attack."

"Are you sitting down?" he asked, "because you are in for a massive shock."

"If you are going to tell me you're getting married, it won't be a shock, so stop panicking," she said with genuine interest.

"No, nothing like that," Rob said, still with urgency in his tone.

"Okay, I'm sitting down now. What is it you need to tell me?"

Fourteen

The news from Rob was indeed shocking. "Let me get this straight, Rob," she said and she related her interpretation of the heart-rending news. "Your mother has a younger sister, Maria, who was going out with your dad's brother, Rhys Jones when she was fifteen. When she first arrived in England, she was living in the Bolton area with an Italian family and was spending weekends in Llandudno with your mum and dad."

"That's where she met Uncle Rhys," Rob continued. "I must have been about two and I always called her Zia Mimi. She conceived a child and didn't tell a soul about it at the time. Several years later, six I think, she told mum and dad her secret, but not before she swore them to secrecy. Zia Mimi was getting married and she had told her fiancé about the child. She didn't want to begin married life keeping secrets from her husband. It was he who advised her to inform Mum in case the child ever came looking for her birth mother. I think she needed to have support from her older sister." He paused and Annie could hear his rapid breathing in those few seconds of silence. "The child, a girl, had been left at St Anthony's Orphanage with a note which said: *Bella Jones – Italian mother, Welsh father,* pinned on her blanket." He sobbed. "Annie, she gave birth on her own in a public toilet, stole a baby blanket from a washing line and wrote the note on a piece of toilet paper to give the child a name. She wanted to leave it with an identity at least."

"Oh my God," Annie cried. "Oh, my blessed Lord!"

Rob kept talking. "When you said you were an orphan, Mum and Dad panicked and felt it better not to pursue the topic further. To be honest, in their panic, they thought you might be Maria's daughter, but they genuinely felt that the best way of keeping a secret was to forget about it and not talk about it at all."

Annie was fitting the pieces of the jigsaw together. "I *knew* at the time their reaction was—what can I say—indifferent," she said pointedly. "Yes, that's it exactly. They were indifferent, rather too indifferent on being told a major fact about my past. I thought they would, at least, have asked about the orphanage even though I didn't mention St Anthony's, but they didn't ask anything at all. They appeared to greet the information I had just revealed with stony silence."

"Can you blame them, Annie?" Rob asked bluntly. "They had been entrusted with an enormous secret..."

"And why have they told you about it now?" Annie was more than curious.

"Zia Mimi does voluntary work at a hostel in Blackpool where she and Zio Nino now live," Rob explained. "They clean the common room, cook meals and often provide clothes for the homeless. This week they were asked to clear the loft of accumulated rubbish...magazines, newspapers, books and the like. They found very old newspapers that had apparently been collected for charity, you know, so much money for so many hundred-weight of paper? A copy of the *Bolton Evening News* dated the day after Bella died, was amongst the newspapers and the accident was reported on the front page."

Annie sobbed quietly. "That is terrible," she cried. "It is heart-rending and traumatic on a lot of levels, and I must say, incredible that the newspaper had been there for so long. It's almost ten years ago! "

"The Lord moves in mysterious ways, Annie. I'm not big on religion, but I think Fate dealt this hand to my aunt." He heard Annie weeping. "I wish I were there to hug you and dry your tears," he told her gently.

"I'm okay," she said. "If only we had known all this earlier when Bella was still with us. Jack took her to Blackpool and she loved it. How could she have known her birth mother lived there? That's so sad, so very, very sad."

"Are you all right, Annie?"

"I think so," she replied through her tears. "I coped with losing Bella; I'll cope with all this."

"That's the Annie I know and love," he told her.

"And I have to ask, where does Rhys Jones feature in all this?"

"He was told when Zia Mimi told Mum and Dad," Rob explained. "He was a sixteen year old boy experimenting with his raging testosterone levels when he was with Maria. He didn't want to accept responsibility so long after the birth and a couple of years later, he emigrated to Canada to cut himself off from the rest of the family. He's none the wiser about what is happening now. Dad doesn't feel inclined to inform him."

"I would have to say I agree, seeing that Bella is no longer with us," Annie said wisely. "Had she been alive, I think she would have had the right to know who her father was."

"Can I ask you a big favour?" Rob asked.

"You can ask, but I'll be up front with you if I can't do it," she stated honestly.

"Would you consider coming to Llandudno to see my parents and Zia Mimi? I know it's a big ask, but when I told them Bella was your best friend, they all said they would like to talk to you." Rob's voice was soft and very gentle. "I know what it will mean to them if you could find it in your heart to share your memories with them."

Annie didn't reply straight away.

"Are you still there, Annie?" Rob asked anxiously.

"I'm here," she replied quietly. "Can I think about it and let you know tomorrow? I need to get my head round all this."

"That's fine," he told her. "We'll speak tomorrow then. Bye for now, Annie."

Annie drove to Llandudno the following Tuesday which was her day off and met with Rob's family at the restaurant. She arrived there at ten-thirty and as the restaurant didn't open at lunchtimes during winter, she knew they would be able to talk uninterrupted.

"Hello, Annie," Giulia Jones greeted her. "You know, Idris, Rob's father, and this is my sister, Maria and her husband, Antonino Rossi. We call him Nino."

"Hello," Annie said as she shook their hands. "I feel very nervous and I think perhaps you feel the same."

Maria Rossi nodded nervously, but did not speak. Her husband, however, took the reins. "We are very grateful to you for coming to meet us," he said displaying his Italian accent laced with broad Lancashire.

Annie breathed in deeply. "I wasn't sure if I could face you all after the recent revelations. I was always the timid one, but Bella was strong and her strength of character helped me tremendously as we were growing up."

Maria looked sadly at Annie. "Was she happy?" she asked timidly.

Annie took another deep breath before she spoke. "In all honesty, she wasn't happy as a child. She felt the whole world was against her and she often misbehaved to gain the attention of the nuns. When I arrived at St Anthony's, she was given the task of looking after me. The nuns thought the responsibility might give her something to concentrate on instead of looking for mischief all the time. In hindsight, that was a mammoth task to give to a child who was only four years old." She smiled. "Bella wasn't a bad child. She gave the impression that she could cope with anything the world threw at her, but I knew her better than anybody and I know that under the hard exterior, there was a very soft heart."

Maria began to weep and Nino put his arm round her. "I was just fifteen," she began. "I hid my pregnancy from everybody. An Italian girl who speak not much English felt very alone. I eat big meals so that people who look after me in Horwich think my swollen belly was from eating too much."

Annie went to take her hand and knelt at Maria's feet. "That probably made her a healthy baby," she said gently. "She certainly turned out to be strong of body and of mind."

Maria continued. "When I go in labour, I go to Rivington on bus. I know orphanage near there. I walk around…"

"You don't have to tell me all this if it's too upsetting," Annie told her gently.

"*Si*, I do," Maria said firmly. "It's the only way I say sorry to my bambino, my baby girl…" She paused and wiped away her tears. "As I say, I walk around for hours and hours. When it is dark, I steal baby blanket and nappy from washing line. The house backed onto road leading to Rivington Pike, I not remember name of road."

Annie allowed her to continue without interrupting.

"When I knew bambino come, I go in ladies' toilets near Rivington Barn and deliver her myself. I cry all through labour and all through giving birth. I push fist in mouth…" She demonstrated to Annie how she used her clenched fist to combat the awful pain. "…and bit it so not to scream…"

"That must have been absolutely terrifying for you," Annie said as she gently squeezed Maria's hand.

Maria sobbed. "I know I have to cut cord and tie it so I take scissors and string in my pocket. She was beautiful. That's why I call her Bella. *Si*, Bella Jones. I give her Rhys's name so she be accepted as British baby," she explained. "I wrote it with lipstick on piece of toilet paper. I need to give her identity."

"Mrs Rossi…"

"Please, call me Maria," the distraught woman said.

"Okay… Maria, I am not here to judge you. If I can be totally honest, I think Bella was sad that you had given her away, but she never talked of hate or condemnation. She only mentioned you once to me with words to the effect that her Italian mother obviously didn't want her. I must say, though, the nuns never encouraged us to seek our birth parents. They told us we might not like what we found, but after today, I can see that they were wrong, in Bella's case at least."

Maria shifted uncomfortably in her seat. "I love Bella. That why I give her to nuns."

"We all know that now," Annie told her gently. "But how could we have possibly known then...almost twenty years ago? Bella had been in St Anthony's four years before I arrived there. She would have been thirty years old now. I truly think that if Bella were here now, she would have thrown a bit of that Italian paddy Sister Agatha once accused her of and then loved you with all her heart."

Both Maria and her sister smiled through their tears and Giulia said, "She got that from my sister. Maria always had a quick temper when she was growing up. Only when she was fifteen did she become quiet and reflective and we didn't know why until she told us her secret several years later."

"After baby born, I come to stay with Giulia and tell her I had very bad—how you say—gastro upset. Nobody questioned it and I recover quick," Maria said to show how she got away with hiding the truth.

"We felt stupid when Maria told us about the baby eventually," Giulia admitted. "How on earth would I have missed all the signs? And we never heard of police searching for a mother. They usually do that, don't they?"

"Maybe the orphanage didn't report it," Nino surmised. "The war was still going on so that could be a reason why. I doubt we will ever know."

Annie let go of Maria's hand, stood up and gave her a hug. "You needn't worry anymore," she said gently. "My only regret is that you never had the chance to get to know your beautiful daughter." She smiled. "I see Bella in your eyes."

"*Grazie mille*," Maria said. "Thank you very much."

"Shall we have lunch?" Giulia suggested.

"That would be lovely," Annie told her.

They sat round the table in the private quarters above the restaurant and Giulia served *antipasto* before chicken carbonara with penne pasta. As they ate, they talked of happier times and Annie related how Bella had fallen in love with Jack. *I won't say anything about the day she died. They don't need to know those details,* she thought. *They only need to know how much Jack loved her.* "Before I leave, I think I should tell you that if you contact Sister Agatha at St Anthony's, I'm sure she will allow you to visit Bella's grave. Mention that you have spoken to me. I don't think she needs to know any details. Compassion is part and parcel of her calling. Nice to meet you, Maria and Nino, and good to see you again, Giulia and Idris."

"Thank you again for meeting us today," Nino offered.

"Not a problem," Annie replied. "I hope it has given you some closure."

"Good to see you again, Annie," Giulia told her. "Take care and safe journey back to Bolton."

Fifteen

When Annie arrived home, she felt drained. She kicked off her shoes and flopped onto the settee. She touched the locket she was wearing around her neck and wondered about her own birth mother. *All the soul searching today has left me feeling empty,* she thought broodily. *Do I want all the hassle of finding the woman who gave birth to me? I was two years old when I was left at St Anthony's. I must have been looked after by somebody for two years.* She shivered. *Oooh, somebody walked over my grave.* Shaking herself out of her reverie, she searched around for the television remote control and found it under a cushion. She flicked on the early evening news. There was nothing in particular to cheer about. The week so far had heralded very little good news. The age of majority had been lowered to eighteen and Karl Marx's grave had been vandalised by anti-Germanic racists. *Silly people,* she thought, *and I'm not that certain lowering the age of majority is sensible. I'm glad I didn't have to vote at eighteen. It was hard enough sorting out what I wanted to do with my life, never mind voting for what was best for the country.* Annie's mind drifted back to her newspaper she had left open on the kitchen bench. *Maybe I should seriously consider the Australian Migration offer. Ten pounds for the fare is really too good to ignore. I could rent out my house for a couple of years and see how I go. Going to Llandudno today on my day off, means I'll have to wait until next Wednesday, but that's okay. I'll go to Manchester next week and suss out what I have to do.*

~ * ~

Two months later, she had made out her application and submitted it to the Australian Consulate in Manchester. Her interview had gone well and she was told that her qualifications would be welcomed by any State Health Authority in Australia. The consulate official was concerned about only one thing. "You will need a passport, Miss O'Shea and for that you need a birth certificate."

Annie's heart missed a beat. "Oh dear," she said dejectedly. "I'll have to see what I can do. Thank you for your time, sir."

"Good luck," he replied with a friendly smile. "Let me know how you go on. I'll keep your information on file and wait to hear from you. I hope I shall be able to add you to the list of ten pound poms."

~ * ~

"...so you see, Reverend Mother, I need to find out as much as possible about my birth mother," Annie implored. "Do you have any information you haven't told me? I have my locket with a picture of me as a baby, well, I think it's me. Other than that, there's nothing."

Mother Superior looked directly at Annie. "You know, Annie, we don't advise that you look for your birth mother. You never know what sort of bad things it might unearth."

"But I'm not looking for my birth mother, Reverend Mother. I just need a birth certificate in order to apply for a passport," Annie told her firmly. "At this point, I'm not certain I ever want to look for the woman who gave birth to me."

"I believe you met the woman who gave birth to Bella," the nun stated sternly.

"I did, Reverend Mother. Did they come to visit Bella's grave? I said you wouldn't mind, but I didn't think they would come straight away. I only saw them a week or so ago."

"They came the day after you had seen them, Annie. Sister Agatha dealt with them and said they were a sweet couple." She shook her head slowly. "I really don't want to know the lengths you went to, to find them…"

"Oh, it wasn't like that at all, Mother," Annie interjected.

"No more on the subject, Annie. I would prefer not to know," the Reverend Mother said firmly. "Sister Agatha has told them they might visit when they want to, but she always takes a softer line than I do."

Annie looked at the Mother Superior through judgemental eyes. *Why do you have to be so cold, Reverend Mother?* she thought as she sat opposite the woman who, rightly or wrongly, had made so many decisions over the years for children in her care. *Please show a little more compassion as becomes you and your position.*

"What I *can* say, Annie, about your own situation," she said coolly, "is that you should go to the Citizens' Advice Bureau. They might be able to help."

"Thank you, Reverend Mother," Annie said. "I'll do that. Thank you for your time."

The Mother Superior smiled condescendingly and Annie noticed.

"Goodbye, Annie. Good luck and God bless you."

"Goodbye, Reverend Mother. Thank you again," Annie replied and made a hasty exit. As she ran to the door, she bumped into Sister Agatha. "My, my, little Annie. Where are you going in such a hurry?"

"Oh, hello, Sister," Annie answered and then slowed down. "I'm going to the Citizens' Advice Bureau to see if they might tell me how to obtain a birth certificate."

Sister Agatha pursed her lips. "Oh dear," she lamented. "Such a mine field to go through, but good luck."

Annie thanked her and went on her way.

~ * ~

"There is now a register of abandoned children, introduced only this year," the advisor told her. "The information on there would be sufficient for you to obtain a British passport."

Annie was perplexed. "Would the Mother Superior know this?" she asked, wondering why the Reverend Mother had chosen to pass the buck.

"Maybe, maybe not," the advisor continued. "All institutions who are involved in looking after orphans and abandoned children have been asked to provide records of every child that passed through their system. St Anthony's will have had the memo, I'm sure."

"Perhaps they haven't had time to go through all the records..."

"Assuming they kept records," the advisor surmised.

"I'm sure they would have," Annie assured him. "I have personal belongings..." She fingered her locket wistfully. "Well, if they kept things on trust, surely they will have kept records as well. I was left there when I was two..."

"You were two years old?" the advisor asked. "Who looked after you until you were two?"

"I have no idea," Annie told him. "I just know my name and I have this locket."

The advisor looked pensive. "If you have a correct name and an approximate date of birth, there might be a way to obtain a birth certificate. You could have applied to Somerset House, but they are packing up to move the records to St Catherine's House as we speak. Services will be suspended during the move."

Annie was completely dejected. "Oh dear," she said sullenly. "I really need to get a passport. Is there any other way for me to apply?"

"I'm sorry. It seems to be bad timing on your part," the advisor told her. "Leave it with me and I'll make enquiries. I have your number on your file. I'll call you when I find out anything."

"*If* you find out anything, you mean," Annie said despondently.

"When," he said firmly. "Don't be a defeatist, Annie. There is always a way when we look carefully."

~ * ~

For the next three weeks, Annie immersed herself in her work. She deliberately saved her days off for when she would be making plans to leave the country. She arranged that Jean, her student nurse, would rent her house with Monty, her boyfriend and would move in at short notice as soon as Annie knew what was happening. "Here I am, making all these plans and I haven't even got a passport yet," she told Jean as they took their break together.

"I feel really sorry for you, Annie," Jean sympathised. "It must be really frustrating."

"I'm used to it, Jean," Annie told her. "Ever since I left St Anthony's, there has been obstacle after obstacle to overcome. Talk about jumping through hoops! Anybody would think we had it easy not having strict parents to contend with, but believe me, I'd rather have strict parents than not knowing who I am."

"Aw, Annie. That's so sad."

Annie shrugged. "Ignore me, Jean. I'm just feeling like the whole world is against me at the moment. I'll get over it. I usually do."

When Annie arrived home after her day shift, there were several messages on her answer machine. One was from Rob who was visiting Bolton and wanted a place to stay. Another was from Shirley saying she was pregnant again and Brian had got a new job as an accounts clerk with the local authority. Another was a call she took regularly from Maria Rossi and the last one was from ...

This is Michael Partington from the CAB. I have pulled in a favour from a friend, Graham Bradbury, who works in Somerset House, now at St Catherine's House. I gave him the little information we had...your full name and approximate date of birth and possible place of birth being Bolton. He has come up with some remarkable details. Please call in to see me as soon as possible.

At first, Annie was struck dumb, but suddenly, she screamed and ran around her lounge like a mad woman. "What?" she shrieked. "Oh my goodness! Oh my dear Lord! Forgive me if I blaspheme, but Jesus, Mary and Joseph, you beauties, you bloomin' beauties."

In her prayers that night, she apologised profusely for her blasphemous outburst and asked the Lord to understand her delight in what she might be finding out as soon as she was able to visit the Citizens' Advice Bureau again.

Annie took her day off that week and was outside the CAB before it opened at ten o'clock. "Good morning," she greeted Michael Partington. "I am so excited."

"So I can see," Michael said as he unlocked the door of his office. "Just sit down while I gather my paperwork."

Annie sat on the edge of her seat and twiddled her thumbs nervously as she waited. When Michael sat behind his desk, she leaned forward eagerly as he flicked through the file. "Here we are," he declared breezily as though he had been looking for it for a long time. "I'll explain it all first and then you can look at it yourself afterwards."

"Thanks," Annie said. "My mouth has gone very dry."

He gave Annie a glass of water, then began. "A search was made in births registered under the name of O'Shea. At first, Graham found twenty Anne Marie O'Sheas, some born before your estimated date of birth and some after. Two of them stood out. He had an Anne Marie O'Shea born in June nineteen forty-two and the second, born on the fourteenth of September of that year."

"Wow!" Annie explained. "If that's me, the nuns were spot on with their calculations, but it has to be a coincidence, doesn't it?"

"I'm as sure as I can be that it's you. The coincidence is too great. The birth was registered by the mother, Victoria Shaughnessy," he paused before he passed on the next bit of information. "...in Donaghadee, Northern Ireland. The father was named as Declan O'Shea. Graham had to contact the Northern Ireland Records Office."

"Oh my goodness," Annie said quietly. "I'm Irish, if that's me. Where do I go from here?"

"Well, you apply for a birth certificate to St Catherine's House," he informed her. "It will cost thirteen shillings and sixpence for standard delivery and seventeen and six for next day delivery. If I were you, I'd go for the next day delivery."

"This is insane," she marvelled. "Thank you so much. I can't quite believe it."

"I am only too pleased to help," Michael said amicably. "It isn't every day we can come up with results like this. If you call Graham on his office number which I'll give to you, he will deal with it personally when he receives your cheque." He grinned. "It's good to have friends in high places."

Sixteen

Annie's passport arrived four weeks after she had received her birth certificate. She phoned the Australian Consulate and arranged to go in with her documents so that her migration might go ahead. She decided to travel by air although travelling by sea was very tempting. She had served her notice and Rob went over to stay with her for a few days before she was due to leave.

"I'll miss you, Annie," he told her. "I will really miss you."

"No, you won't, Jonesy," she quipped. "You only see me once every blue moon these days."

"That doesn't mean I won't miss you," he rejoined. "I haven't found anybody else to love since you. I once told you, you were unique and it's true. How many other girls would still see me after splitting up?"

"It's because we are friends, good friends, and I can't think of any reason to be enemies just because we aren't sleeping together anymore," Annie pointed out. "I still love you, Rob, but not in the intimate way."

"Oh damn and blast it then," he joked. "And here I am thinking I might just get my leg over one last time before you leave."

"Don't push your luck, Jonesy, or you won't stay over at all," she told him. "And before you say it, I know you're only speaking in jest."

"Well, I insist I take you and your enormous amount of luggage to the airport on Saturday," he told her forcefully.

"I'll agree to that," she said. "Now let's get organised for Thursday's farewell gathering."

~ * ~

Thursday came and went. The farewell open house took place from lunchtime onwards. People popped in, had some nibbles and a glass of wine or a cup of tea or coffee and then left to get on with their day. Hospital staff visited in their breaks and Shirley and Brian arrived with their offspring early in the afternoon.

"I'm happy for you, Annie," Shirley told her. "I envy you being fancy free and able to do all these adventurous things."

"Oh, come on, Shirl,"Annie rebuked her. "You love being a wife and mother and I know you wouldn't change it for the world."

Shirley laughed. "Some days I would, when I have two screaming kids, one with a gastro upset and Brian coming home from work having picked up a flu bug from the guy on the next desk. I love my life, but some days I yearn for a bit of adventure."

"Keep in touch with me when I have settled in one place and I'll relate everything I'm doing so you might at least dream," Annie suggested.

"Oh I will," Shirley agreed and then she called to her husband, Brian, "Are you ready for the off, Mr Edwards? We need to hit the A55 before five o'clock, otherwise we'll be in all the works traffic."

Jean and Monty arrived in the early evening. Annie was pleased to see them. "I am so grateful to you two," she told them as they dumped several large suitcases in the vestibule. "I have vacated my room for you. The bed is made and the drawers and wardrobes are empty. If you'd like to take your stuff upstairs, you can unpack and settle in while I make us a cup of tea. I'm afraid I'll have to leave the changing of the guest bed for you to do when I've gone. You know Rob, don't you?"

They nodded and made their way up the stairs. "Thanks, Annie. You're a star."

"Where are you going to sleep, Annie?" he whispered.

"I'll make up a bed on the settee," she told him. "It won't be the first time I've slept down here."

"You can't do that," Rob insisted. "You have a twenty-four hour flight to contend with tomorrow, not to mention the time difference of nine or ten hours. You need a good night's sleep. Let me sleep on the settee and you have my bed in the guest room."

Tea made, Jean and Monty joined them. "Make yourself at home, won't you?" Annie said. "I'll be going to bed soon. I have to be at the airport at seven o'clock in the morning and that means getting up and being ready to leave by six."

"I think we'll have an early night too," Jean told her. "I'm on earlies tomorrow and Monty has to catch the eight o'clock train to Preston. He has an assessment to make on the new Preston Guild Hall. It's supposed to be built and fully functional by the end of April nineteen seventy-two, but it will all hinge on what he finds tomorrow."

"Sounds interesting," Rob observed.

Monty shrugged. "All in a day's work," he said matter-of-factly. "I can't foresee any delays at this point."

"Sorry to be a party pooper," Jean said apologetically, "but it's time for bed. Come on, Montgomery, up the dancers!"

"Goodnight all," Monty said and winked. "See you in the morning."

Annie washed up the teacups and Rob dried and put them away. Annie yawned. "Time for bed," she said. "Come on, Roberto. All your dreams will come true tonight. It's going to be a long time before we'll see each again after tomorrow."

Rob looked wide-eyed at the young woman he had adored since the first time he saw her in the dinner queue. "What are you suggesting, Sister O'Shea?" he asked with a glint in his eye. "And what about our friendship not being intimate?"

Annie smiled. "I'm suggesting I throw all my morals out of the window tonight and I'll say a friendly intimate goodbye to you." She took his hand and led him upstairs.

~ * ~

They arrived at the airport in good time. Annie looked at Rob as her luggage was checked in. "I hope I don't have to pay excess luggage fees," she said nervously.

The check-in officer looked at her questioningly. "Are you emigrating?" she asked.

"I am," Annie replied. "Have I got too much luggage?"

"You would have if you were a tourist, but emigrants are allowed thirty pounds extra plus hand luggage that you carry onto the aircraft," the check-in officer told her. "I'll check these cases right through to Sydney."

"Thank you," Annie said and turned to Rob. "I'll go straight through to passport control, Jonesy. I don't like long goodbyes." She hugged him affectionately. "Please forgive my promiscuity last night. I had an urgent need to feel close to you. I surprised *myself* by the way I came on to you."

"You don't have to ask for forgiveness, Annie," Rob told her. "No man would refuse an offer like that from a beautiful blonde Audrey Hepburn look-alike. You surprised me too, but I won't hold it against you. I think we merely fulfilled a need in each other at that particular time. After all, we are consenting adults and there are no strings attached."

Annie looked into his eyes with the love that only a true friend would understand. "You know, Jonesy, you are the best friend I have ever had...after Bella, of course. Your cousin would be delighted that I shed the shackles of prudishness and propriety if only for one night. Keep in touch occasionally, won't you?"

With a final hug, Rob was gone and Annie took the next step into the future and into the unknown.

Seventeen

The thirteen hour flight to Singapore from Manchester was uneventful and extremely tiring. The constant drone of the engines prevented Annie from sleeping and the over-enthusiastic man sitting next to her didn't stop talking for most of the flight. Landing at Changi Airport was a welcome relief. She found the shower rooms and decided to take advantage of the facility during the four hour transfer time. Feeling somewhat refreshed, she found a café where she had freshly baked croissants and several cups of coffee. She stretched her legs by walking around the pristine airport and admired the floral displays that added an outdoor atmosphere to the enclosed space. When her Sydney flight was announced, she strolled to the gate and joined the queue to board. After another eight hours plus, she landed in Sydney and was herded with a few other ten pound poms towards a mini bus which took them to their accommodation in Villawood, some twenty-five kilometres from the city.

They found themselves destined to stay in migrant hostels on arriving in Australia. Hostel conditions left a lot to be desired, but Annie was given single accommodation providing only basic living arrangements. It was a converted Nissen hut used during the war and the huts were only intended to accommodate migrants for a short time, until they were able to save money and buy their own home. They didn't pay rent until they had secured jobs, and food was also provided.

Annie looked around the sparse room that was her living room and bedroom combined. She had a small bathroom and separate toilet. Flopping onto the bed, she held her head in her hands and whispered, "Oh my Lord. What have I done?"

Feeling too tired to unpack after the long flight, she wandered down to the dining area and found other people looking strained and confused. The cafeteria arrangements were better than she expected and she joined the queue of people waiting for lunch. "Hello, how are you?" she greeted the two people in front of her who looked at her non-plussed.

The guy behind her tapped her on the shoulder. "They can't speak English. I think they're Czechoslovakian."

"Oh, I see," Annie said. "Maybe we should help them."

"I don't think I can," the guy told her. "I have a pregnant wife and two other small children to take care of. Four weeks in and I'm still wondering if we are going to survive in this set up."

"It is a bit daunting, isn't it?" Annie responded. "I didn't expect it to be like this either."

"Where have you come from?" the man asked.

"I'm from Bolton in Lancashire. And you?"

"The other side of the Pennines," he answered. "Leeds."

They collected their food and Annie looked around for an empty table.

"Come and sit with us, if you don't mind whinging children. They seem to get tired in this heat. That's my wife and kids over there."

They wound their way through crowded tables and managed to find an extra chair for Annie to sit with the family. "I'm Stan Derbyshire and this is my wife, Sarah."

"Hello, I'm Anne Marie," she said. "Pleased to meet you." Her thoughts made her smile. *New life, new name. I'll introduce myself with my proper name from now on although I guess I'll still be Annie underneath.*

"And I am so pleased to meet you, Anne Marie," Sarah told her. "All I've heard since we landed are foreign people speaking foreign languages. It's good to hear English without an accent, if you see what I mean."

Annie laughed. "I'm sure we'll be fine once we settle in. And who are these little people?"

"This is Oliver. He's six and this is Louisa. She's three and a half," Sarah explained. She patted her bulging midriff. "This little one is due in just over three months. I'm due on Christmas Day, but I'm hoping it's early or late. I don't mind which so long as I don't have to miss Christmas Day with the children. It's going to be strange anyway with being away from the rest of our family in Leeds, and having Christmas in the sun will be different, won't it?"

"To be honest, I haven't got as far as thinking about Christmas," Annie said. "My priority has to be getting a job."

"That was mine too," Stan told her. "And we have to find a school for Oliver. We need to know where we'll be living before we are able to choose a school. Hopefully, he'll be able to make friends before they break up for the summer holidays."

"Summer holidays in December seems very odd, doesn't it?" Annie remarked.

"It does, but I quite fancy a Christmas picnic on the beach, don't you?" Sarah said dreamily. "I'm dying to see Bondi Beach."

"It does sound wonderful, but I'll be happy just to have a job and my own house or flat by Christmas," Annie stated. "I can't see me enjoying living here in this hostel for too long, can you?"

"Not at all," Stan agreed. "I started work three weeks ago. I'm an electrician so I managed to get a job the day after we arrived. There are a lot of properties being built to accommodate all us poms. What do you do, Anne Marie?"

Annie smiled. "I'm a midwife," she told him.

He and Sarah laughed. "Ah well, we'll have to stay close to you then, won't we?" Stan declared.

"Please let us know when you get settled," Sarah added. "I feel better already knowing we've met a midwife before we've even found somewhere to live."

~ * ~

By the end of September, Annie had secured a job at the Royal Hospital, her British qualifications being well received since nursing training and education were under re-structuring to enable nursing staff to organize their work days more adequately. With her salary being paid each month, she was able use a portion of her savings transferred to her new bank account from the National Westminster bank in Bolton, to put a deposit on a terraced house in Stanmore. As planned, by Christmas of nineteen seventy-one, four months after after she had first stepped onto *terra australis*, she had moved into her new home. She had written to Jean and Monty to ask if they would send her belongings she had packed into boxes before she left. When the boxes arrived, she found delight in seeing her bits and pieces again and the personal effects made her Australian house feel more like home.

She wrote to Shirley as soon as she had settled in: *I have bought a little house just a short bus ride from the hospital, although I plan to buy a car in the new year. I have settled very well in my new job. The nurses and midwives are very friendly and to be honest, they seem to ask my advice on things, especially post-natal care. I feel very privileged.*

I have been out with one of the doctors a couple of times. He's nice, but I can't see it going anywhere. We only seem to have work in common. He's sporty and likes surfing and Australian Rules football. I'm not sporty at all other than liking to walk along the fabulous beaches at Bondi and Manly. There are some wonderful walks at places with unpronounceable names like Wooloomooloo. The Royal Botanic Gardens are beautiful and I've walked around them numerous times. I never tire of trying to remember the names of native plants. They are so different from British plants.

Sydney is a terrific place and I'm happy I chose to come here. The Harbour Bridge is magnificent, majestic and any other adjective you might choose to describe this wonderful piece of engineering achievement. When the Opera House was opened last year, that too became synonymous with Sydney's iconic stature. I just love the city. I have started a bucket list as there is just so much to explore in this vast country.

The family I met when I first arrived have settled in Annandale which is not very far from where I am living. I delivered Sarah's third child, a little boy, on Boxing Day. She had desperately wanted their first Christmas in Australia to be spent on the beach, but baby Ryan had other ideas.

I'm going to visit a high school next week to promote careers in nursing. I must be doing something right to be selected to do this. I'm sure I'll be nervous. I'm not used to speaking in public, but I'll prepare well and then hope for the best.

Hope all is well with you and the rest of the Edwards family. Start saving so you can come to see me. I know you would love the lifestyle. It is so relaxed.

~ * ~

A week later, Annie prepared for her first presentation to high school students and found she enjoyed the new experience. When the principal's report was sent to her supervisor, she was asked to take on the role of education mediator on a regular basis. "It will only be once or twice a year in each school," the supervisor told her. "If we speak to year eleven and year twelve students, we'll give careers advice to prospective nurses as well as to university applicants."

"That's good," Annie told her. "The year twelve students I spoke to wanted to know what courses were available at uni. I need to find out more about that as back up to what their teachers tell them."

"Maybe we can organize a meeting with Southern Cross and the University of Sydney to begin with," the supervisor suggested. "We can see how that goes before we arrange anything else."

~ * ~

Annie's first year in Australia flew by. She decided that her life there by far outweighed her life in Bolton. She wrote to Rob telling him she thought she would make her future in Australia: *There are*

Most of Annie's working hours were spent in the labour ward and she had several student midwives under her wing. The hours were long, but she had time-off pro rata. Towards the middle of the final school term, her presentations took over and she spent less time on the wards. The day she went to the school farthest away from the hospital, she drove her own car there. Previously, the hospital authority had provided transport for her, but it was much more convenient to drive there herself.

She arrived early and the principal suggested she should go to the staff common room and talk to the teachers who were responsible for the subjects relevant to nursing and the medical profession generally. "That would be great," Annie told him.

"This is Sheila Carson, our Head of Science," the principal said. "I'll leave you in her capable hands until it's time for you to meet the students. Sheila, meet Anne Marie."

"Thanks, Mr Cuthbertson," Annie said. "Hi, Sheila. Good to meet you."

"How are you?" Sheila asked.

Having become used to the Australian's way of greeting each other, Annie replied, "I'm good thanks, and yourself?"

"I'm good," Sheila answered and true to form, she concentrated on Annie's mouth as she spoke. It made Annie smile.

"Did I miss something?" Sheila asked amicably.

"Oh, sorry. No, you didn't miss anything," Annie explained. "I am so used to people concentrating on my mouth to lip read because of my accent. It makes me smile. I hope I didn't offend you."

"Not at all," Sheila assured her. "We have teachers here from all over the world, all with different accents. Your English accent is easy to understand. I tell my English colleagues that how they speak is actually the proper way. We Aussies are the colonials, after all!"

"I like that," Annie said. "Now I won't feel quite so self-conscious when I open my mouth."

After being introduced to most of the science teachers, Sheila took her to the drama studio where she was about to meet students in small groups. As they approached the door, an extra-curricular drama class was winding up and leaving the studio. Annie stood back and held the door open as the group left. The teacher gathered his books from the table and went to leave.

Time seemed to stand still. "Annie? What on earth are you doing here?"

Eighteen

Annie paled and felt sick. She stood there in dumb silence and stared at the man before her. He too was visibly shaken and the awkward silence between them was noticed by Sheila Carson, who broke the uncomfortable atmosphere that was developing. "I don't know what is going on here, but may I suggest you two catch up at recess? We all have work to do before then."

Annie anticipated the most unnerving two hour question and answer session with students who, fortunately, were very mature. When they saw Annie, they were very understanding of her indisposition. "It's all right, Miss O'Shea, if you are not well," said one of the seventeen year olds.

"Would you like to sit out this session and we can see you when you feel better?" said another.

Annie took a deep breath. "I'm fine," she told them. "I'll just work my way through it."

"Would you like a glass of water?" asked the girl who was first concerned about Annie's welfare.

"That would be good," Annie responded. "Thank you."

~ * ~

David Anderson was waiting outside the drama studio door when the bell rang for recess. He was holding two mugs of coffee and when the students had left, he entered and placed the cups on the table. Making sure the door was closed, he turned to Annie, a look of absolute apprehension on his face. Annie folded her arms and pressed her lips together in an effort to overcome the anxiety that was building up inside.

"What is going on?" David asked. "What in God's name are you doing here, Annie?"

"I have every right to be here, same as you," she said, trying to combat the trembling that was taking over her whole body.

"But you're a nurse, I presume, unless you took up a different profession when you left Half Way House," he stated, his cheeks burning with embarrassment.

Annie found her confidence returning. "Well, that's for me to know and for you to find out," she hissed, surprising herself with the disparaging tone of her voice.

David looked totally crushed and Annie noticed. "This is not the time and place for us to air our differences," he said. "Can we meet up somewhere, sometime, somehow?"

Annie couldn't hide her amusement and she laughed. *If I hadn't seen Westside Story, those words would mean nothing to me,* she thought as she silently reprimanded herself. *I almost feel like bursting into song. I must try to control myself. I am being decidedly immature.*

"Did I say something funny?" David asked, irritated that Annie was making fun of him and belittling him. "I don't like being made a fool of."

Now it was Annie's turn to be disgruntled. "Be careful, David," she warned. "Don't go down that road unless you are prepared to justify yourself and your past actions."

"Are you free tomorrow, or do you work Saturdays?" he asked cagily.

"I am free tomorrow afternoon, but I'm not sure I want, or need, to give you the time," she told him.

"I can't make you meet me if you don't want to, but I would like a chance to talk to you," he said quietly. "We used to be capable of being honest with each other."

Annie looked at the man who had stolen her heart and then broken it into little pieces without so much as a by your leave. "I need to talk to you too, David, but it might not be very pleasant so we should both be prepared for the backlash that might occur."

David shrugged. "Can I pick you up about two o'clock tomorrow then?" he asked. "Where are you living?"

"I'll meet you at Circular Quay," she suggested. "I can get the train into the city and I presume you can do the same."

David didn't argue. "Okay, I'll be at the news kiosk at two o'clock." He went to hug her, but Annie stepped back, deliberately putting herself out of his reach.

~ * ~

On Saturday afternoon at two o'clock precisely, Annie found David waiting for her by the news kiosk as arranged. He looked awkward as she approached and he made no attempt to give her a welcome hug after the rebuff the day before. "Hi," he said tentatively. "Thanks for coming. I wasn't sure you would turn up."

"You should know me better than that, David," Annie told him coolly. "I don't let people down when I've made an arrangement."

David breathed in deeply. "I guess I deserve that," he said resignedly. "I'm not trying to sugar-coat what I did. Shall we go to find a place at The Rocks where it's quiet, or would you prefer to walk round to Darling Harbour? There are lots of benches there overlooking the harbour. We might find a vacant one." He was waffling and he coughed to hide his nervousness.

"Let's just walk," Annie answered quietly. "We really aren't here to admire the view, beautiful though it might be."

David stuck his hands in his pockets to avoid touching Annie. His thoughts drifted back to when he had first tried to hold her hand. *She was so petrified of any ramifications that would develop from openly touching each other.* "Dare I ask again what you are doing here?"

"I'm doing the same as you, I think," she said, still feeling tense about the whole incredible situation. "I took advantage of the ten pound pom scheme. It was too good an opportunity to miss. I thought

I had come to a sort of impasse in my life and I wanted to see the world a bit after I had been totally restricted from travelling as I was growing up. You know my history, David, so surely you can understand why I'm here."

"I do understand and, yes, I thought the opportunity was too good to miss too," he stated.

Annie cut straight to the chase. "Why didn't you contact me?" she asked bluntly. "The last words you said to me as you left Bolton on the train were *I love you*. What happened in Exeter that completely consumed you and made you forget all about me? I waited and waited for a whole year before I decided you weren't worth waiting for. What sort of a person does that to the girl he said he loved?"

"It took me a long time to find a permanent place to stay," he said making some effort to try to explain what happened without it sounding like an excuse. "I dossed down with new friends I made when first arrived in Exeter. I lived out of my suitcase for a couple of weeks until I was fortunate enough to be offered a bed in a shared house."

"But that doesn't explain why you totally cut me off," Annie complained.

"No, it doesn't," he admitted sheepishly.

"Did you meet another girl?" she asked.

"I met several girls, but I didn't fall in love with them," he offered. "When I said I loved you, I meant it..."

Annie gasped. "So why did you cut me off...cast me aside like an old boot? You shock me, David, especially when you had suffered being abandoned by your father. Surely you could have worked out how I would feel."

David looked uncomfortable. "I am finding this very difficult, Annie, so please bear with me. I have to give you the truthful explanation and I'm struggling to find the right words."

"You're not married, are you?" she asked.

"Please, Annie, let me do this without interruption, or I might not be able to say what I need to tell you."

They reached Darling Harbour and found a bench far enough away from the hubbub of local weekenders and tourists so as not be distracted. Annie sat and stared out across the harbour without looking at David at all. David sat at an angle so that he might see Annie's reactions as he spoke.

"I will repeat, to begin with, when I said I loved you, I meant it...I genuinely meant it. You are—were—my dearest *girl* friend and I had never been close to anybody like I was close to you. I loved you and I loved that you loved me. When you asked me to make love to you after Bella died, I couldn't do it and I told you it was the wrong time for us to lose our virginity. That was true." He paused to collect his thoughts. "It was true, to a point, which will become clear in a moment. When I arrived in Exeter and I hadn't found somewhere to live, a friend, Jason, was very helpful in finding me a place in his shared house. He was doing the same course as me and we struck up a close friendship..."

"Oh my dear Lord, David," Annie murmured. "What are you going to tell me?"

"Please, Annie, don't interrupt," David implored. "This is important. Jason liked me—a lot—and I discovered I liked him too. He was happy with his sexual preference and he recognised that I was in denial about mine..."

Annie's jaw dropped. "You needn't go any further, David. I really don't need to know all the gory details."

"I'm sorry I let you down," he said sincerely. "I was between a rock and hard place..."

"Too clichéd, David," she quipped. "That's what you always told me when I succumbed to using clichés to explain how I felt."

David managed to smile. "Pan calling kettle, I suppose." And they laughed again together. "Are you still mad at me, Annie?" he asked warily.

"Yes, I'm more than mad, I'm livid," she told him firmly, but managed to smile as she spoke. "If you felt as close to me as you say, why was it so difficult to tell me the truth all those years ago?"

David took a deep breath and blew it out slowly. "I know I ought to have been honest with you from the start, but I was scared you would hate me and not understand. I took the easy way out and the longer I left it, the harder it became to contact you."

Annie looked at David and felt his pain. "Oh, David," she murmured. "All this is such a shock to me and yet, strangely, I don't feel any animosity towards you anymore. I have never had to consider homosexuality before, but at this moment in time, all I feel is acceptance and compassion. I believe love is love whether it's between a man and a woman, or between two people of the same sex. I loved you with all my heart. You were my first love and when you broke my heart into little pieces, I eventually accepted that these things happen in our lives. It helped in some small way to my social adjustment after St Anthony's. Bella had shown me how to build an invisible wall around myself as protection against any adverse outside influences. It worked for as long as I wanted it to."

David moved in and gave her a hug and she allowed him to hold her close for a minute or two without saying a word.

"I often think of Bella and how she would have dealt with the things life throws at us," Annie reflected. "In all honesty, she and I never discussed homosexuality, but I think she would have been philosophical and said, '*each to his own.*'"

"I guess she would," David agreed. "Do you think you might find it in your hopefully-now-mended heart to forgive me, Annie?"

She took his hand and squeezed it gently. It was obvious they had the same thought simultaneously and they both laughed as David proclaimed in his most nun-like manner, "Remember girls, never allow skin on skin or you will live to regret it!"

"Can I just ask you one thing?" Annie queried.

"Ask away," he replied. "Ask as many things as you like."

"When you asked me out all those years ago, were you aware of your feelings for boys at that time?"

He smiled. "No, I wasn't," he told her. "I liked you, I really liked you and when I kissed you, I felt butterflies in my stomach probably because it was the beginning of some sort of sexual activity for me. Being so close to a girl triggers testosterone levels to increase, an involuntary reaction if you like. It was only after you asked me to make love to you that I became aware of something different occurring. Jason brought out those feelings almost as soon as I met him."

"So why did you come out here?" Annie asked. "Is Jason still in the picture?"

"We came out here together," David informed her. "Nobody seems to mind two guys sharing an apartment. We have made lots of friends, both straight and gay. We lead a very happy life. Jason is teaching in a private school and you know where I work." He gave her a questioning look. "And you? Is there a husband, or any boyfriends in tow?"

"Not at the moment," she revealed. "Since I started work at the hospital, I've been out with one of the doctors from the hospital a couple of times, but I don't think he's the one. I'm okay being single, though. I too have made friends both male and female, so I'm not lonely."

David gave her another hug. "I'm glad we're friends again, Annie O'Shea," he acknowledged. "I'd like you to meet Jason. He knows all about you."

"I'd like that," she told him. "I have to ask you though, changing the subject, how did you go on in those flippin' hostels when you first arrived?"

David looked at her with eyes wide open. "It was like being back at Half Way House," he said, "Queuing up for our food ..."

They parted on very good terms. "I'll call you, Annie," he told her.

"And I'll call you," she said.

Nineteen

Seeing David again helped to confirm that true friendships never die. They met up once a week, sometimes at David and Jason's apartment, sometimes at Annie's house. Annie usually took friends along and gradually, they formed a close knit group of like-minded people who discussed topics both frivolous and serious. It was when they were at Annie's house one evening that David asked, "Have you ever thought of looking for your birth mother, Annie? We talked about it once a long time ago and you said you might think about it once you had qualified in nursing and had a permanent job."

"I think about it sometimes, but it's difficult to know where to start," she told him. "We found Bella's parents..."

"You did what?" David exclaimed. "How did you do that?"

Annie explained about the Rossis and about Maria Rossi in particular. "What is definitively incredible is the fact that I had been going out with Bella's cousin and we never knew they were related."

"That's unbelievable," Jason commented.

"It is...was," Annie agreed. "I still keep in touch with the Rossis. Maria says she feels close to Bella when she talks to me. She phones maybe once a month, sometimes more if she feels the need."

David looked puzzled. "If they are called Rossi, why was Bella's name Jones?" he asked. "Did the nuns give her that name?"

"No, Maria did," Annie told him. "Bella was the product of rampant teenage testosterone and the father didn't know anything about the pregnancy. Maria had kept it a secret from everybody. That's no mean feat, is it? It was only when she was about to marry, she told her then fiancé so that she wouldn't begin married life keeping secrets from her husband. Bella's father was Maria's brother-in-law's brother, Rhys Jones. Maria's sister was my ex's mother."

"Oh wow, that's complicated, but I think I've got the gist," David offered. "How traumatic would that have been for Maria? And while there was war raging all over the world too."

"It was very traumatic for Maria and she gave birth alone in public toilets, stole a blanket off a washing line and left the baby at St Anthony's," Annie continued.

"How sad," David whispered. "but how did Bella get her name?"

"Maria wrote *Bella Jones, Italian mother, Welsh father* in lipstick on toilet paper and put it inside the blanket with the baby. She admits her **naïvete**, but she thought Bella would be accepted without question if she had a British father. We were always told by the nuns that we shouldn't search for our birth parents, because we might not like what we **found**," Annie informed them. "I questioned the nuns' teaching when I met Bella's birth mother and I was sad for her because she would never know her daughter. As for my parents…"

David noticed Annie's demeanour. "What's wrong, Annie?" he questioned. "Why are you so pensive? I know you when you suddenly go quiet."

Annie smiled. "I already know the names of my parents," she divulged.

David nudged her playfully. "So you've been stringing us along, have you, Annie O'Shea?"

"Not really," she replied. "I needed to get a passport to come out here and I originally had no birth certificate…"

"And you have one now?" David asked excitedly.

"I do," she continued. "A very kind gentleman in the Bolton Citizens' Advice Bureau managed to obtain it for me. My mother's name was Victoria Shaughnessy and my father's Declan O'Shea."

"So you're Irish then." Jason stated matter-of factly.

"I am to be sure," Annie told him. "I was born in Donaghadee, Northern Ireland. I was two years old when I was left at the orphanage. Somebody, presumably Victoria Shaughnessy, looked after me for two years. Goodness only knows what happened to make her leave me on St Anthony's doorstep. Why would an Irish woman be in Bolton? She obviously wasn't married if she registered my birth in her maiden name and then named the father as O'Shea."

"There's a bit of a mystery there for sure," David observed. "I'm fascinated, Annie. If you decide to look for the two people who gave you life, count me in. I'd love to play detective with you."

"Thanks, David, but I'm not ready for that yet," she informed him. "Maybe when I go back to the home country next year..."

"You're going back?" David gasped. "To live? I thought you loved it here."

"Calm down, Anderson," she said laughing. "I'm going for a holiday, although I don't think it will be much of a holiday with all the flying around I'll have to do to catch up with friends. I know at least three people who will make demands on my time and two of those will want every intimate detail of everything I've done in the past few years."

"But you'll come back, won't you?" David and Jason said in unison.

"I'll definitely be back," she reassured them. "Life in Bolton can't possibly compete with what I have over here."

David gave her a hug. "Who'd have thought we'd be in Australia at all, Annie?" he offered. "When I made you that first cup of coffee under the eagle eye of Mrs Constable, we would never in our wildest dreams have envisaged this."

Annie laughed. "No, we wouldn't, but I dread to think what Mrs C would think of you and Jason. She had a really hard time preventing girls and boys from going out together. We never did find out why she was so concerned about Bella and Jack and later, you and me going to the cinema together. Something must have gone badly wrong in her youth for her to have such hang-ups about young love. I wonder how many other young couples she warned about the consequences of being together."

"Ah well, I think I can shed some light on that," David revealed.

"What?" Annie cried. "Have you obtained some inside information?"

David went to sit on the sofa and patted the seat next to him for Annie to join him. "Do you remember John Lawton who was at Half Way House?" he asked.

"I do, although I never got to know him," Annie replied. "He left to go to uni soon after I arrived."

"He did medicine and did his internship at Guy's Hospital in London," David informed her.

"Wow, that's posh," Annie commented.

"Well, he wrote a letter to me and sent it to Half Way House after we had left," David continued. "Mrs Constable forwarded it to me."

Annie was quick to jump in. "Hold on, Anderson," she complained. "How come Mrs C knew your address and I didn't?"

"Get off your high horse, O'Shea," David scolded playfully. "She phoned admin at Exeter uni and traced me that way."

"I wish I'd thought about that at the time," Annie pondered. "Mind you, knowing what I know now, you probably wouldn't have replied, would you?"

He winked. "Probably not at that time," he admitted. "But I struck up a sort of pen-friendship with John and we reminisced quite a lot in our letters."

"I can understand that," Annie told him. "It's not as though either of you had families to turn to."

"Anyway, Mrs Constable had written to John several times," David went on. "According to John, she seemed to want to unload all her worries on him, maybe because he was a doctor."

"Get on with it, David," Annie urged. "You are keeping me in suspense. I'm dying to know what she did to be so intense about boy and girl relationships."

"Well, one time when she wrote..."

"Oh for goodness sake, Anderson, stop procrastinating and tell me," Annie protested.

"When she was fourteen, her mother found her in bed with a boy," David divulged.

"Oh my dear Lord," Annie whispered. "No wonder she was hell bent on stopping the young people in her care from making the same mistake. I'm glad I'm not her daughter, though."

"She never had children, Annie," David informed her. "In fact she told John she never married. She just took the title *Mrs* to give her credibility in that job." He paused. "And to give the impression she was worldly-wise in all things sexual."

"And she actually said that to John, did she?" Annie asked seriously.

David laughed. "No, *I* said that," he admitted. "That's my assessment of her obsession with frigidity."

"Ooooh, you bad boy!" Annie said, laughing with him. "But it does explain why she was so clear about not forming boy and girl relationships for her to watch developing. No wonder she grilled us when we were always together."

"Poor woman," Jason observed. "She must have been driven to distraction at times."

"Not by David and me, Jason," Annie assured him. "We were the model house guests."

That day, Annie left the apartment of her friends with a happy heart. David always had the gift of making her feel good.

Twenty

Annie decided to apply for Australian citizenship when she had been resident there for three years. Her decision to stay permanently had been easy, and with Jean and Monty being settled in her house, it seemed the natural progression to allow them to buy it if they so wished.

"Are you kidding?" Jean shrieked when Annie put the idea to her.

"No, I'm not," Annie told her. "It would make life so much easier for you and for me. Will you get a couple of valuations and then we'll come to some agreement?"

"Not a problem," Jean enthused. "We can't thank you enough, Annie."

The valuation and sale went through without a hitch and Annie relaxed in the knowledge that she no longer had responsibilities back in Bolton.

Every now and again, she met up with Stan and Sarah Derbyshire and their ever increasing family to compare notes on how they were adjusting to life down under. "I'm an Australian citizen now," Annie told them after she had been sworn in. "Are you two going to have the operation?" she asked, laughing at what she had just said.

"What operation?" Sarah questioned. "I wasn't aware we had to have surgery in order to become Australian."

"Don't be daft, love," Stan interjected. "It's the Aussie way of saying you are fully entitled to be called an Australian. If you ask about the operation, they'll tell you it's a lobotomy to make you conform to the Aussie way of life."

"How gross," Sarah muttered.

"We will apply for citizenship soon," Stan told her. "Two of our kids are Australian because they were born here. We need to be consistent as a family and anyway, I think it shows respect to the country that has accepted us with open arms to live here. Having Australian passports for us all will make it much easier when we travel back to the homeland for a visit to our families."

"My sentiments exactly, Stan," Annie agreed. "I'm planning a trip for June and July. I thought I'd escape the cooler weather here in winter, for the British summer."

"Good luck with that then," Stan said tongue-in-cheek. "We have winter days here that are hotter than British summer weather."

"I know and I fully intend to gloat about that when I return," Annie told him.

~ * ~

Planning the return trip to Bolton was very exciting for Annie. She would be there for four weeks, which would give her time to catch up with Shirley and Brian and their three children, with Jean and Monty and with the Rossis. She would stay with Jean and Monty initially and they were getting married while she was in England, so she would be the perfect house sitter while they went on honeymoon.

Jean and Monty met her at the airport and drove her to Bolton. It was early in the morning and with the ten hour time difference between Australia and England, Annie was well and truly jet-lagged. "Living ten hours twice over cannot possibly be good for the system," she said wearily as she kicked off her shoes. "I am absolutely drained."

"We'll have a cup of tea and then you can go and have a lie down until you feel normal again," Jean suggested. "Tomorrow, Monty and I are on earlies, so you can stay in bed as long as you like."

"Thanks, Jean, but I'm so excited about seeing everybody again, I don't think I'll sleep much anyway," Annie told them. "I've heard it's best to try to keep going to get your body clock back to normal... you know, being awake in the daytime and going to sleep at night. I'll struggle through somehow."

"Your car is still in the garage," Jean told her. "I've driven it every now and again to keep it road worthy. I kept the paperwork up to date, too and your MOT is current."

"Thanks for that, Jean," Annie said gratefully. "Before I go back to Oz, I'll transfer it over to you. It's not worth a lot, but it will keep you going for a while."

"I'll pay you for it, of course," Jean told her.

"You won't," Annie said firmly. "Like I said, it isn't worth much, and take it as being part of the sale of the house. I have a car in Sydney and it's pointless keeping one here for if and when I come back. Please accept it as a gift with my thanks for all you have done for me."

After spending the first week of her holiday seeing most of her Boltonian friends, Annie visited Bella's grave at St Anthony's. Sister Agatha welcomed her with open arms. "Thank you for calling to see us, Annie," she said. "We heard you had gone away to live in Australia. God bless your spirit of adventure."

Annie smiled. "It's the best thing I ever did, Sister. Australia is a wonderful new country, a land of opportunity for those who are prepared to embrace it. I wish Bella could have gone with me."

Sister Agatha looked sad. "I do too, Annie. That poor wee soul needed a new start and to be loved. We tried..."

"I know, Sister, I know," Annie agreed. "We all did, but Bella was happy in the end. We have to believe that or our faith would mean nothing."

"You are a wise child, Annie O'Shea," Sister Agatha offered.

Annie gave the nun a hug and asked, "May I go to visit Bella's grave? I have flowers and plants to leave for her."

"Certainly you may," Sister Agatha told her. "Bella's friend, Jack Spencer, comes once a month and leaves flowers."

"Does he?" Annie exclaimed. "That's wonderful!"

"He's a nice young man," the nun said. "He's married now and he brings his lovely wife with him. They have a little girl and they named her Annabella. Now, isn't that lovely?"

"Beautiful," Annie said. "Please remember me to him when you see him again."

She took a bouquet of petunia flowers to symbolise their friendship and placed a sprig of rosemary in for remembrance on Bella's grave. With Sister Agatha's permission, she planted lilies-of-the-valley around the edge of the plot to make sure there was happiness surrounding Bella at all times.

She sat at the foot of the grave and prayed in a whisper. "Dear Lord, please make sure my sister, Bella Jones, is happy in your care. Tell her I love her and I will never forget her. Make sure she knows her mother comes to visit her often and ask her to smell the flowers I have brought for her today. I chose the petunias specially, because they make up the colours in the magic carpet I always wanted her to ride with me. They have beautiful, bright colours that bring joy to the heart." Annie wiped away the tears that were trickling down her cheeks. "Oh Bella," she murmured. "I miss you so much." She placed a small pebble on the headstone to show she had visited the grave. "Rest in peace, my darling friend."

~ * ~

Maria and Nino Rossi had moved from Blackpool to Abergele so as to be closer to the Joneses in Llandudno. Annie drove over to visit them during the third week of her holiday. "You stay with us," Maria invited when Annie called to tell her she would drive over to see them.

"Thank you, Maria, but I just have to stay at the St Tudno Hotel again," she told them. "I don't know how long it will be before I'm back again and I have so many fond memories of my first visit to North Wales. I'm going to try to re-live some of them."

"*Nessun problemo*," Maria said. "No problem, but I disappointed."

"I'll spend some time with you, of course," Annie assured them. "I hope to catch up with Rob, too, and that will give me a chance to see the marble church at St Asaph. I have never been in it so it is an absolute must for me on this trip."

Maria went quiet and Annie noticed the awkward silence. After a moment or two, Maria spoke. "Annie, Rob engaged to girl he meet when he stay at Windermere cottage…"

"Oh?" Annie responded. "He kept that one quiet, but it's okay. I'm pleased for him. Will he meet me, do you think? I understand if he can't, but it seems a pity if we don't meet while I'm here. I wondered why I hadn't heard from him for a while. I hope he will be very happy. Has he set the date for his wedding yet? Do you really think he'll see me?" Her thoughts were confused. *Why am I gabbling? I must sound like a blithering idiot. Slow down and talk sensibly.*

"I tell him you're in Llandudno," Maria told her. "Perhaps we can all have a meal at Casa Nostra with Giulia and Idris. I know they be pleased to see you."

"That will be nice," Annie said, desperately trying to sound enthusiastic, but thinking she had failed miserably.

~ * ~

She met with Shirley, Brian and their brood in Penmaenmawr. Their house overlooked the Irish Sea and Shirley was keen to show Annie around. "On a clear day, we can see Anglesey and Puffin Island," she told Annie. "Mind you, I can count the number of clear days we get on one hand, but I love it here and the kids are happy living by the sea."

"It's lovely, Shirl," Annie agreed. "You have done really well. A good husband and three beautiful children and another one on the way, I see."

"Aw, that's not fair, Annie O'Shea," Shirley whined. "How did you know? We only just found out ourselves."

"Pregnant women have a glow about them, Shirl. You should know that," Annie reminded her. "I'm dealing with pregnant women all the time. I know these things."

"Well, we've got Brian's mum and dad to look after the kids for a couple of hours so we can take you out to lunch," Shirley told her. "We'll take you to The Ship at Red Wharf Bay. You'll love it."

"That sounds great," Annie replied.

The lunch was indeed wonderful and afterwards, Brian went for a walk round the bay. "I'll give you girls time to talk about woman stuff," he said as he left. "I'll be back in about half an hour."

Annie and Shirley sat in the sunshine on a bench facing the bay. Shirley was the first to speak. "How are you, Annie love?" she asked.

"I'm good."

"Hey, this is me you're talking to, Annie O'Shea," Shirley scolded. "There's something on your mind, I can tell." She nudged Annie playfully. "You're not the only one with psychic powers, yer know!"

"Blimey Moses, Shirley," Annie grumbled light-heartedly. "Can't a girl think in private these days?"

"Not when it's you and me, she can't," Shirley told her. "Come on, out with it."

Annie pondered for a moment. "I'm beginning to think I'm never going to find that special someone to love," she divulged. "You remember I told you about David who went off to uni and never contacted me?"

"I do," Shirley told her. "The rotten ..."

"He's in Australia and we bumped into one another quite unexpectedly."

"You are joking, girl!" Shirley shrieked. "What happened?"

Annie related the whole story. "...and in spite of everything, we are such good friends," she revealed. "He still understands me and I can rely on him to be there for me if I need him."

"That's amazing," Shirley replied. "*You* are amazing. I don't think I could be so magnanimous after the way he just left you dangling, not knowing what was going on."

"It's in my genes, I think," Annie said resignedly. "I started my life as far back as I can remember as an abandoned child. Maybe I'll just tough it out for the rest of my days. My friend Bella always said we started with nothing, so we'll finish with nothing."

"That's not true for you, though, is it, Annie?" Shirley protested. "You are made of stronger stuff. You've got a good life and you've carved that out for yourself. You keep your chin up, girl. Everything comes to her who waits."

~ * ~

The meeting with the Rossis and the Joneses took place the day after she had been to Anglesey with Shirley and Brian. They met for dinner at the Casa Nostra. The restaurant was full, but Idris Jones left his chef in charge so that he might join the rest of the family. "This is wonderful," Giulia said as they tucked into their *antipasti*. Annie noticed they were sitting at a table for eight but three seats were not taken. Giulia saw her looking at the empty places and explained, "We were hoping Rob and Kathryn would be joining us. They were supposed to be bringing Kathryn's brother to make up the numbers, but it looks like they can't make it."

Annie smiled. "Oh, that's a shame," she remarked with affected disappointment. "It would have been nice to see Rob before I leave. Never mind. Just wish him and Kathryn all the best and tell him I'll write to him when I get back." Her heart was beating wildly in her chest and she tried desperately to maintain her composure.

When Annie returned to the hotel for her last night in Llandudno, she flopped on the bed and gasped, "Oh my dear Lord. Please don't put me in a situation like that again." Her thoughts were more troubled than before. *I really wanted to see Rob. I have so much I want to say to him, but I'm as sure as I can be that he won't want to hear it now he's found somebody else to love.* She closed her eyes tight and felt tears welling up inside. "Oh no," she sobbed. "What am I doing?" *My heart is broken again. I thought I didn't love Rob enough to include him in my life, but the mere fact that he has replaced me with Kathryn really hurts. I thought I didn't have a jealous bone in my body, but it seems I have a whole skeleton of them. I'm jealous and that's the truth. Dear Lord, let me live in the knowledge that Rob is happy with his life. I wish him well, I really do, but...* She undressed and got into bed without washing her face or cleaning her teeth. *I don't want to look in the mirror tonight and see what a wretch I have become.*

Sleep eluded her and when morning came, she was grateful that she would soon be flying back to Sydney and leaving Great Britain behind forever.

Twenty-one

After Mass on the last Sunday of her trip, she drove to Rivington to visit Mrs Constable at Half Way House and was disappointed to find it had closed down and was now a hospice for the terminally ill. Nobody there seemed to know what had become of Mrs Constable so she drove to St Anthony's wondering if the convent had closed too.

"Come in, come in, little Annie," Sister Agatha greeted her. "How lovely to see you again."

"Hello, Sister..."

"I'm acting Reverend Mother now, Annie," she corrected. "Dear Reverend Mother Ursula passed away three weeks ago, shortly after you came to visit Bella's grave." She crossed herself as she said, "May she rest in peace."

Annie was taken aback, but crossed herself also and whispered, "You should have told me, Sister, but I can still remember her in my prayers. May she rest in peace." She took a deep breath to contain her emotions. "I'm so sorry to hear of her passing. I wondered why I didn't see her at that time, but I just assumed she was busy. Come to think of it, I didn't see any children either. What has happened to them?"

"We are in mourning, not only for the Reverend Mother, but for the closing of the convent. We have no children now, Annie. Our numbers dwindled after you and Bella left and funding dried up, so sadly we had to close the orphanage."

Annie looked at the nun who had been her close advocate during her childhood. "Where will you go, Mother?" she asked earnestly. "And what will happen to Bella's grave and all the other graves in the cemetery?"

"The cemetery will be untouched, so you needn't worry about Bella. There are only six of us left here now," the nun explained. "We will transfer to a retirement home in Leeds. We are all growing older by the minute. Do you remember Mrs Constable from Half Way House?" Annie nodded and the nun smiled. "She went to live with a friend in Devon. She too is growing older, but you look well, little Annie. Life in Australia must suit you."

"I think it does, Mother. I think it does."

~ * ~

Annie's plan was to spend a couple of days in London before flying out of Heathrow to Sydney. She had a well-orchestrated itinerary that allowed her to see all the iconic landmarks with one day left to visit St Catherine's House. She went there on the morning of her last day.

"I'm sorry Miss O'Shea, but records for Northern Ireland are kept in Belfast," the clerk told her.

"Is there any way I might access them while I am here?" Annie asked. "I leave tomorrow and I hoped I would find out at least if my parents were alive or dead. I know my mother was in Bolton in June nineteen forty-four, but I was born in nineteen forty-two in Northern Ireland."

The clerk pressed her lips together and tapped on the desk as though to trigger some thought. "I'll look in the war records to see if any of your parents were involved in active service," she said. "I'll just be a moment." She disappeared into the storeroom and returned with microfilm which showed war records from nineteen thirty-nine onwards. "I'll show you how to work the machine and then you can browse through at your leisure," she said and she showed Annie to a desk in the corner upon which was the microfilm reader.

"Thank you," Annie said as she removed her jacket and hung it on the back of the chair. "I feel quite nervous, not knowing what I might find on here."

"Don't worry too much about it and it will be easier for you to cope with whatever you find," the clerk reassured her. "Just relax."

"I'll try," Annie replied. She inserted the film into a contraption the likes of which she had never seen and flicked though at lightning speed until she came to names beginning with O. *Ogden, O'Haloran, O'Leary, O'Mara, Ormerod, O' Shea.* Her heart skipped a beat. *Aiden, Brendan, Bryan, Colum, Cormac, Davin, Dec...* "Oh my word," she whispered. "What does it say?"

Declan O'Shea 874926; Corporal; First Battalion Royal Irish Fusiliers; France; Missing in action. May 1944.

"Oh my dear Lord," Annie whispered. She pieced together in her mind bits of the scenario that must have led to her being left at St Anthony's. *If my father were missing, presumed dead, my Irish mother perhaps had nobody to turn to in Bolton. The mystery is... what was she doing in Bolton and is she still alive now?*

Annie returned the microfilm to the clerk who asked, "Did you find anything?"

"I did," Annie told her. "The only thing is, I need to try to follow up on what happened to my mother after June nineteen forty-four. Is there any other way I might find out about her?"

"Census records would be the best way, but unfortunately, we can't access the information on those," the clerk informed her. "Church or parish records might help."

"Looks like I've hit a wall," Annie reflected. "Never mind, I'll see if I can contact people when I arrive home. Thanks for your help anyway."

"My pleasure," the clerk told her. "You might try to look up ships' passenger lists. A lot of people left the country when the war ended. Don't hesitate to contact us in the future if we can be of help."

The following morning, she arrived at Heathrow three hours before her scheduled flight as required and once she had checked in and cleared passport control, she found a comfortable seat away from the madding crowd and started a journal of her trip while it was fresh in her mind. By the time her flight was called for boarding, she had enjoyed reminiscing in detail. The entry for the time she spent in North Wales was left for later. *I need to call on Bella's strength to find my solace regarding that affair of the heart,* she thought as she gathered up her hand luggage and headed for the boarding gate. *At the moment, I can't even find the courage to mention his name.*

Twenty-two

Annie was scheduled to go back to work a couple of days after her return to Sydney. David phoned her as soon as she set foot in her home. "How was it, Annie? Did you miss us? Did you give my regards to Bolton?"

"It was a great holiday and maybe I missed you a little bit, but I have so much to tell you," she informed him. "I'm really tired after the flight and I have to start back at work on Monday morning, so I'll call you when I've recovered."

"Come for lunch tomorrow," David invited. "I know you won't feel like shopping or cooking or going to a restaurant, so that's settled. We'll see you tomorrow at twelve noon for one o'clock. No discussion."

"Okay, bossy boots," she conceded. "I'll see you then." Afterwards, she phoned Sarah to arrange a visit on her day off, before unpacking her case, loading the washing machine and flopping on the sofa to catch forty winks. She woke with a start at six o'clock in the evening and cursed herself for interfering with the management of jet-lag. "Silly person," she cursed. "Now you'll not sleep tonight." She busied herself with drying the washing in the tumble dryer and ironing while she caught up with the Australian news on television. Not much had changed in the few weeks she had been away, but in October,

Australians were going to be introduced to bank cards, little rectangles of plastic that would revolutionise the way in which money might be spent. "Hmm," she pondered. "I wonder where that will lead." By one o'clock the following morning, she began to feel tired again and went to bed happy in the knowledge that her body clock had started to return to normal.

Lunch with David and Jason the following day was just as enjoyable as she'd expected it to be. "You two are my bestest friends in the whole wide world," she oozed after her second glass of merlot.

"Don't you drink anymore," David warned. "You have to drive home and be ready to work tomorrow."

"I'm fine," she assured him. "Just ply me with water from now on."

Jason placed a jug of water on the coffee table. "There you are," he said. "Help yourself. When are we going to hear about your trip? You have only told us about the flights so far. Surely they weren't the highlight of your holiday." He laughed and nudged her into action. "Come on, spill!"

Annie made herself comfortable on the sofa. "Well," she began, "For your information David, Mrs Constable has gone to live with a friend in Devon..."

"Male or female?" David asked, laughing at his memories of the uncommonly frigid woman.

"I have no idea," Annie told him seriously. "And please don't go down that road again. There are some things I would rather forget."

David squirmed in his seat, "Sorry," he offered. "No offence meant."

"I know, and none taken," Annie continued. "Half Way House is now a hospice for the terminally ill and the orphanage has closed. That, in my humble opinion, isn't a bad thing, because there were lots of things going on there which were downright oppressive. Thank the Lord I'm not scarred for life. I could quite easily have become a total social misfit had it not been for you, my dear friend. At least you had lived in a home, rather than an institution all your life. You had a better perspective on life than I had until I met you."

David leaned forward and patted her knee. "I don't think I can take all the credit for that," he conceded modestly. "You gained a lot from Sister Agatha in an introverted sort of way, didn't you?"

Annie screwed up her nose. "I have never looked at it that way, but you could be right. Sister Agatha had her own way of drawing our attention to what it would be like after we left St Anthony's."

"I think we all help each other," Jason added. "I had a good family life and David has educated me on things I never knew happened outside my own little world. I needed that in order to understand what contributes to personality and characteristics. Now you are here, Annie, you give everything a different dimension that is invaluable to me as a teacher, so thank you for coming into my life."

"Aw, Jason, that's lovely. Thank you," Annie said as she brushed away the tears that had suddenly filled her eyes. "We are all different, that's for sure. I'm beginning to think I am not normal as far as relationships go. I wish I were able to find that special contentment in being with another person. I find it so difficult to commit, because..." She stopped abruptly and looked down at her feet while she collected her thoughts.

"Out with it, Annie," David urged. "Hanging on to something like that will only tear you apart if you allow it to eat away at you."

"I really try not to think of the person who gave birth to me. I want to believe I was conceived out of love, but she abandoned me when the going got tough and I can't forget that," she revealed. "When I get close to someone, I push them away, because subconsciously I think they will leave me. I do need somebody in my life, I freely admit that, but unless I can overcome this selfishness that consumes me when I feel somebody is trying to take away my independence, I will never find the one special person who will love me forever."

David went to sit by her side and put his arm around her. "I want to help you, Annie, but I don't know how."

"You already help by listening to my sob story," she told him, "But if I don't tell you all this, I'll go mad."

"We're listening," Jason said. "Just talk to us."

"Rob and I were together for three years," she divulged. "He was everything I wanted and still want in a man—caring, understanding, gentle, considerate—and he loved me, truly loved me. He knew all about my background and he helped me in so many ways to accept what I had become since St Anthony's. He often went out of his way to make sure I would feel at ease. I love him…" She stopped again to regain her composure. "Look at me," she cried. "I'm a complete mess just talking about him."

"That's okay, Annie," David reassured her. "It's only us and it will go no further."

"When I bought my first house," she continued, "I wouldn't let him buy with me, all because of this stupid dream I had of owning my own home, *my* home, not anybody else's, not even Rob's who I loved with all my heart. How ridiculous is that? He wouldn't even stay the first night with me in that house because I had certainly made it clear to him that it was *mine*, not *ours* and definitely not *his*."

"But didn't you say you saw him before you came to Australia?" David recalled.

"I did and guess what! I slept with him the last night before I left! How cruel is that? And he didn't hold it against me. He just said we had fulfilled a need in each other." Annie began to weep again. "I'm sorry," she apologised. "I feel such a wimp."

"Stop running yourself down, Annie," David advised. "No-one is perfect."

Annie sniffed and dried her tears again. "Anyway, I didn't see him when I was in Llandudno. I wanted to, because I had a lot to get off my chest. I met up with his parents and with Maria and Nino, of course. We had a meal at the restaurant and there were three empty chairs at the table. Giulia, Rob's mum, said she had hoped that Rob and his fiancée, Kathryn, would join us and they were bringing Kathryn's brother to make up the numbers…" She looked wide-eyed at David. "How the hell am I supposed to feel when he wants to pair me up with his bloody fiancée's brother?"

"How do you know that's what he was doing?" Jason asked

gently. "Making up numbers at dinner doesn't necessarily mean pairing up afterwards."

"I know that and I'm ashamed now that I allowed it to cloud my judgement, but it did show me something about my character," she admitted. "I'm a bloody good actress! I smiled and gushed my way through it until I got back to my hotel room and then I collapsed in tears on my bed vowing that I would never again put myself in a situation like that."

David took her hand. "But you still love him, don't you?"

"I do, truly I do, but I've blown it," she concluded. "I'm thirty-two years old and destined to be a lonely, frustrated old maid for the rest of my days."

"Don't talk like that, Annie," David scolded. "Thirty is the new twenty and look at you! You are beautiful...well, you are when you've not spent an hour crying. You'll pick yourself up and start all over again." It was David's turn now to stop abruptly. He looked directly at Annie. "And I know what you are going to say."

Annie laughed as they said in unison, "Too clichéd, David, too clichéd."

Twenty-three

Going back to work was therapeutic for Annie. Making sure her ante-natal and post- natal classes were up to date after her holiday kept her busy and she had four mothers due to give birth that week. Her visits to David's school were now very pleasant and they had lunch together as they had when they were studying at Half Way House. David was very interested in Annie's search for her birth mother. "Tell me how far you got when you were back in the home country," he asked. "We never got around to discussing that when you came back."

"That's because I was a blubbering mess about Rob," Annie admitted. "I did find out something at the records office, though."

"Anything significant?" David enquired.

"It could be," Annie informed him. "It seems in nineteen forty-four, my father, Declan O'Shea, was missing in action, presumed dead."

"Oh my goodness," David said sympathetically. "No wonder the poor woman couldn't look after you."

"That's what I thought," Annie agreed. "The biggest mystery is, what was an Irish woman doing in Bolton two years after giving birth to me in Donaghadee?"

"Yes, I agree," he remarked. "Maybe she married after the war and took a different name. That would make it more difficult to find her, but so much more interesting."

Annie looked pensive. "The clerk at the records office suggested I look at church records and ships' passenger lists. The best information would be on a census, but that information wouldn't be accessible until twenty fifty-one." She laughed. "I think I'll be pushing up daisies by then."

David gave her hand a squeeze. "Why don't we try writing to the priests at the local Catholic churches in Bolton to see if they will check their records for the marriage of Victoria Shaughnessy?"

Annie suddenly looked scared. "What if she isn't alive anymore?" she asked in fear and trepidation. "It's a distinct possibility. Many war widows died of broken hearts."

"And many were strong and determined not to let Hitler dictate what should happen to them," David stated with authority. "Judging from your strength and resilience, O'Shea, I would put money on the fact that your mother was one of those people who survived and moved on."

"I would hope so too," Annie agreed, "but if she were strong and resilient, why didn't she come back to St Anthony's to get me after the war? That's another burning question, isn't it?"

David thought for a moment. "I suggest we write to the parish priests and that way, they will provide us with any information they have, be it marriage or death records."

"Okay, that sounds good," Annie concurred. "With their help and a bit of divine intervention, we should be able to piece things together. Suddenly, I'm quite excited about finding out who I am. Previously, I wasn't particularly bothered one way or the other."

"We'll get our heads together at the weekend if you're not working," David said. "Hopefully we'll have some news before the end of the month."

~ * ~

Annie greeted a new first time mother who had registered in her ante-natal class. She was a quietly spoken young lady, but with an air of confidence about her. "Come in, Mrs Kirkwood. May I call you Jill? I'm Annie. Pleased to meet you."

Mrs Kirkwood smiled. "I'd feel more comfortable if you call me Jill. Mrs Kirkwood sounds so formal. I love the way medics and their patients are on first name terms. It seems to give me more confidence in my doctor and ..." she paused. "... and nurse, of course. My mother told me that never used to happen."

"Thank goodness for progress then. We'll be best friends before this little one comes into the world. We'll just go through your records before we begin the class. You are how old?"

"Twenty-nine; thirty in October," Jill told her. "A bit old for a first time mother, I guess."

"Not really," Annie replied. "At least you've lived a little before you have your children. Now let me see; estimated date of confinement is February fourteenth. How lovely, a Valentine's Day baby. How romantic! Now, just one more thing before we begin the class ...does your husband want to be involved in the birth? There is a movement in relaxing the rules to enable fathers to be present when the baby is born. What's his name?"

"Andrew. I'll ask him when he comes home from work," Jill told her. "What I know of him, he might be a bit squeamish. He nearly fainted when I had stitches in my knee." She smiled knowingly. "That's men for you."

"No need to rush him in that case," Annie replied. "Maybe if he comes to a few of the—how shall we say—easier appointments nearer the time, he might warm to being present at the birth of his child."

Jill joined three other ladies in the class and they were made aware of the importance of relaxation during labour by lying in the recovery position and feeling totally relaxed. "Mind over matter. Think of something you enjoyed...a holiday, meeting your husband." She paused deliberately. "The first time you made love..."

"Whoa there, Annie," said one. "I'll make that the second time if you don't mind. I had a slightly better idea of how to respond then!"

Her comment was greeted with laughs all round.

Annie continued undeterred. "We all know and accept that giving birth will be very painful, but by the time your baby comes, you will automatically breathe away your pain."

"We hope," another lady quipped.

"But you will, I promise you," Annie assured them.

After leaving them in a relaxed state of body and mind for half an hour, Annie returned to the class. "All right, ladies, time to go. I'll see you all next month, except you, Amy. I'm expecting you to have your baby before then."

"Me too," Amy rejoined. "The other four came early so I see no reason why this one should be any different."

When Annie went home and removed her uniform, she realized she hadn't worn her badge. It was still on the dressing table where she'd left it the night before. She shrugged as she thought, *I broke a rule today, but nobody noticed, so not to worry.*

~ * ~

One month after she had written numerous letters to the Catholic priests in Bolton, she had heard nothing. "This is so frustrating," she complained to David.

"Parish priests have more than correspondence to deal with, Annie," he responded. "You should know that, good little Catholic girl that you are!"

"Well, out of a dozen letters we sent, you'd think we'd have had one or two replies," Annie muttered.

"I have to agree," David conceded. "We'll just have to be patient. You never know, out of the blue you might just receive the news you want hear."

"I love that you're so positive, David," Annie told him. "I am consumed by negativity at the moment. I really am trying to be positive like you. I have to admit, though, I blow hot and cold about the very idea of coming face to face with the woman who is my mother."

"For goodness sake, Annie," he implored. "Put your trusting hat on for now. We'll meet whatever news comes with either joy or stoicism. That way we will be prepared for any outcome."

Annie hugged her friend and kissed him on the cheek. "Thank you for always being there for me, David. I don't know what I would do without you."

~ * ~

The ante-natal class for Jill Kirkwood came on Annie's day off so Sister Carole Norbury deputised. "I'll see you today, but Annie will be here next month. I know you are her lady—we don't refer to you as patients—you have probably noticed that. We always think that a patient has something wrong, but pregnant ladies are mostly very healthy."

"I noticed that straight away," Jill informed her. "Will you please pass on a message to Annie for me?"

"I will," Carole said.

"Please tell her my husband will be present at the birth," Jill said smiling. "I didn't think he would, but I think he felt very proud when I said he could be there at the nitty-gritty stage."

"That's great," Carole acknowledged. "I'll put it in your record so she'll know when she sees you next."

~ * ~

When the next monthly appointments came round, Annie was pleased that Andrew Kirkwood had agreed to be present at the birth. "We'll hopefully see him during your final four weeks while we prepare you for your imminent birth," she told Jill. "He will be shown how he might help you through your labour. His contribution will be very much appreciated by us as well as by you."

"Thanks, Annie," Jill answered and found herself staring at Annie's name badge. "Is that your name, O'Shea?" she asked.

"It is," Annie said. "Anne Marie O'Shea for my sins." She laughed at her little joke.

"That's amazing," Jill declared. "My maiden name was O'Shea. What a coincidence!"

"Isn't it?" Annie agreed. "I wouldn't think we're related though." She was taken completely off guard. *What the ...? Don't get involved in a conversation about heritage, for goodness sake. I'm not up to that just now.* "Were you born here?"

"I was," Jill confirmed. "I was born in Perth. How my parents ended up in Perth is a crazy story, crazy and complicated. Maybe I'll tell you sometime."

"Maybe," Annie said cautiously. "I'm sure there are lots of interesting stories about coming out here. Still, for the moment, let's concentrate on you. I'm here to look after you and deliver your parents' grandchild. We'll just focus on that, I think."

"Of course," Jill said. "I'm sorry if I distracted you from the job in hand."

"Not at all," Annie replied. "See you next week. Sessions will be weekly now that we are approaching the final four weeks."

Twenty-four

Nothing was heard from any of the priests in Bolton. "I can't believe that none of them has had the decency to reply even if they could find no information," Annie complained.

"I think we should take it as being a certainty that Victoria Shaughneesy did not get married in Bolton," David said resignedly. "Maybe she moved on as soon as she left you at St Anthony's. I guess we should try looking at other ways of tracing her."

"I have absolutely no idea where else to start looking other than passenger lists like the records officer suggested," Annie replied. "She might have more information at her disposal. She said she would help if I needed her to."

"Let's sleep on it, Annie," David suggested. "A problem always seems less of a problem when you wake up in the morning."

"I'm happy with that just now," she told him. "I have several of my ladies due to give birth in the next few days. I'm going to be working very long hours if they all decide to produce at the same time."

"I thought hospitals were more organised than making you do overtime," David stated. "How can you be totally in charge if you are tired?"

"We keep going on auto-pilot," she answered. "You really don't notice how tired you are until you stop. As regards searching for my birth mother, it isn't my priority at the moment. I do want to find her if possible, but I've been without her for thirty-two years. A few more weeks won't hurt."

~ * ~

Jill Kirkwood went into labour two days before her due date. When she arrived at the hospital, the contractions were coming every five minutes. "You weren't wrong about it being painful," she breathed.

Annie smiled. "I know, but just do as we tell you and we'll make it as pleasant as possible. It went in there so it has to come out."

Andrew grinned and squeezed Jill's hand as he whispered, "It went in a lot easier than it's going to come out, didn't it, darl?"

"Behave," Jill scolded. "You can have the next one and then you'll know what pain is." She breathed in deeply and blew out forcefully as another contraction overwhelmed her. "I wish Mum were here," she groaned.

"It's surprising how many of my ladies want their mums when they are in labour," Annie commented as she examined Jill. "I think you'll be a few hours yet. Let me know if it becomes unbearable and I'll give you some pain relief."

"I'm hoping I can do it without pain relief," Jill stated, determination in her tone. "But then again, I might just..." She breathed in deeply again as another pain consumed her. Four hours later, Jill and Andrew Kirkwood became the proud parents of a bouncing baby boy, Michael Joseph, on February fifteenth nineteen seventy-five. Jill's parents flew in from Western Australia the following day.

~ * ~

Annie was on the late shift that day and arrived at the hospital just after visiting time finished. As she parked her car, a jovial couple were getting into their car parked a few spots away from Annie's. "Just imagine, Dec," the lady said happily. "We are grandparents. I can't believe it."

Annie stopped what she was doing as she went to get her bag out of the boot. *Did I hear that correctly?* She looked at the couple's car as it pulled away, her expression one of complete puzzlement. *I must be going out of my tiny mind. Get a grip, girl.*

When she entered the ward, Jill and Andrew were bathing Michael and getting him ready to go to sleep after his evening feed. "I'm pleased to see Daddy learning the ropes," Annie called as she was opening the door of her office.

"Me too," Jill said, "although he hasn't had the joys of changing a dirty nappy yet."

"Hey you," Andrew rejoined. "I intend to be a hands-on daddy so I'll pull my weight, changing nappies included."

"I'm glad to hear it," Annie told him.

"I think he might have to take a back seat while my parents are here," Jill added. "You should have seen them drooling over the baby this afternoon."

"Well, he's their first grandchild, isn't he?" Annie remarked. "That is, unless you have siblings who beat you to it."

"Yes, you're right, Michael is the first," Jill confirmed. "I have a brother, Sean, who is ten years younger than me. He's travelling in Europe at the moment."

"There's a big gap between you and your brother then," Annie observed.

"There is," Jill responded. "Mum thought she couldn't have any more children after so long."

"It happens sometimes," Annie agreed. "Women occasionally confuse the symptoms with the onset of menopause."

Jill nodded. "Yes, but Mum is still quite young. She was only in her thirties when she had Sean. She's fifty now."

"Will you be in tomorrow, Annie?" Andrew asked. "Maybe you can meet the doting grandparents when they visit tomorrow afternoon."

"I will be in," Annie told him. "I have to make sure you have all your instructions before you take Michael home."

"Great," Andrew said with a smile. "Maybe you can say hello then."

~ * ~

It was Annie's day off the following day, but it was in her work ethic to be present when her ladies left the hospital to take their babies home. She arrived at the hospital at two o'clock in the afternoon in order to make sure Jill and Andrew had their complete instructions before they left. She was out of uniform because she was there unofficially.

"Wow, you look nice," Jill told her as she arrived on the ward. "You didn't come in on your day off just for us, did you?"

Annie smiled. "Well actually, I did," she said. "I always make sure my ladies and babies know that I am here if they need me. I have a box of goodies for you, too. It's full of little things for new parents and it contains an A to Z of parenthood. I think that's invaluable."

"Oh thank you," Jill replied, and looking closely at Annie, she said, "What a beautiful locket! Look how the silver shines against your black top and I love the gold heart in the centre. It's so eye-catching."

Annie smiled and gently touched her prized possession. "Thanks. I love it too. I'll just get your leaving gift…" She leaned over the crib to take a peek at the little child who was fast asleep and totally unaware that he was about to take the next big step into the big wide world.

"Oh, here are Jill's parents now," Andrew announced. "Stay and say hi to them, Annie."

Annie looked up. "Hello," she greeted them. "Pleased to…"

Mrs O'Shea's eyes stared at the locket and her hand went to her mouth. Mr O'Shea paled and grabbed hold of his wife's arm trying to stop her from falling over. Annie clutched the locket to her chest and stood rooted to the spot, unable to breathe for a moment or two before she ran to her office, closing the door behind her. She picked up the phone and paged Carole who was there within minutes.

"What's going on?" Jill asked. "Annie has disappeared and Mum and Dad look like they've seen a ghost."

Declan O'Shea led his wife to a chair by the bed and eased her down to sit on it before she fell over. He, himself, was shaking and he sat on the edge of the bed. Carole asked a student nurse to bring some water for the clearly shocked couple. Jill and Andrew were confused. "What is going on?" Jill asked again. Her parents couldn't speak.

Carole took charge. "You get the baby ready for leaving and I'll just have a word with Annie." She went into the office and found Annie in a state of shock. "What on earth is the matter, Annie? This isn't like you at all."

"I think I have just come face to face with my birth parents," she bluntly informed Carole.

"Oh my goodness, Annie," Carole exclaimed. "I had no idea. I didn't know you were adopted."

"I wasn't adopted, Caz. I was abandoned!" she cried. "What am I supposed to do now?"

"I don't know, Annie, but I think you are going to have to talk to them. We can't leave them out there. They look in total shock," Carole said. "Shall I take them to the day room and make sure they have some privacy?"

"Yes, that's a good idea," Annie agreed. "I know I have to speak with them. What I'm going to say, I have absolutely no idea. I'll just take a few minutes to get my emotions under control and then I'll join them. Ask Jill and Andrew if they will please give us half an hour or so."

Annie's thoughts were yet again running riot. *This is insane. How on earth can this have happened? It doesn't make sense.* She looked at herself in the mirror. Her eyes were wild and her face flushed. "Calm down," she told herself quietly. "Take a deep breath and stay in control. You are the nurse here. You are trained to deal with all eventualities."

She walked slowly down the corridor to the day room and found Victoria and Declan O'Shea sitting side by side on the sofa. They looked completely overwhelmed with what was happening. Annie closed the door quietly and went to sit in the armchair adjacent to the sofa. She managed to smile at the confused couple. "I think we have a lot of talking to do, haven't we?" she said gently. "And before we start, I would like you to know that I am not here to judge you. I have questions, obviously, but because of this..." She tapped the locket lightly with her fingertips. "...I know that the decision you made to leave me at St Anthony's must have been very difficult for you."

Declan O'Shea sat upright and began to speak. "Victoria was only seventeen when she fell pregnant with you," he explained. "When she told her parents, they threw her out and told her never to darken their door again. I was eighteen and determined to make sure she wasn't alone. We lived with my parents until she had you and then we packed what few belongings we had and got on a boat to Liverpool."

"How did you end up in Bolton when you landed in Liverpool?" Annie asked.

"We hadn't told anybody we were leaving," Declan told her. "In short, we ran away. We figured Liverpool would be the first place they'd search if anybody should go to look for us, so we got on the first train we saw at the station and decided to go wherever it took us. The end of the line was Bolton. We rented a room in Horwich and I got a job at Horwich Loco Works. We were building tanks during the war. It was a good job and gave us enough money to live and to look after you properly."

"Did neither of your families send out a search party?" Annie enquired. "They must have been curious to know where you were, at least."

"Our brothers had all been called up so with the war going on, they didn't look for us at all," Declan explained. "It was in nineteen forty-three when my conscience got to me and I joined the army. I had to leave Victoria on her own to look after you..."

"...and that's when it all started to go wrong," Victoria rejoined nervously. "He hadn't long finished his training when he was sent to France and it must have been about six months after that when I received a letter saying he was missing in action, presumed dead."

"I knew this," Annie cried. "When I had to find my birth certificate to get a passport to come to Australia, I found out your names and I read about the 'missing, presumed dead' too. I realized then it was no wonder you had to do what you did."

Victoria O'Shea let go of her husband's hand and spoke quietly, her Irish accent adding poignancy to her tone. "I know I have to say I'm sorry, so very, very sorry for what I did. It was the worst day of my life when I left you. You were crying and I was wailing too and that only made you worse. I placed you on the doorstep and rang the bell, all the time telling you not to move." She began to weep softly. "You were a good girl. You always did as you were told, but I was dreading that you might just run after me calling out *'Mummy.'* Why would you do that when you had never disobeyed me before? I ran down the drive and hid behind the wall until I knew you were safe."

"It was Sister Agatha who answered the door," Annie told her. "She was nice...in a nun kind of way."

"I had no job, no money and no partner. I knew I couldn't pay the rent, nor buy food to feed us both," Victoria murmured. "I had no choice but to try to give you a better life without me."

"I understand," Annie whispered. "But how did you end up in Australia?"

Declan rejoined the conversation. "I was injured in France and they put me on an Australian hospital ship. I don't know whether it was a mistake or not, because everything was chaotic at the time, but I finished up in Perth. I wrote to Victoria as soon as I was able and told her where I was. She had gone to live with her sister back in Belfast."

"I only got the letter when the lady who we'd rented the room from in Horwich forwarded it weeks later. As I'm sure you can imagine, I couldn't believe it. I thought he was dead."

"This story goes better and better," Annie marvelled.

"As soon as the war ended, the Australian government introduced the assisted passage for British people to emigrate and I asked Victoria to join me over here. We got married almost as soon as she landed."

"I'd got a job at the university in Belfast, just housekeeping," Victoria added, "but it was easy to save the ten pounds for the trip and I sailed into Fremantle after six weeks at sea." She paused before she asked, "Were you happy, Anne Marie?"

Annie moved in her seat to make herself comfortable. "I have to be honest and tell you that I was never truly happy until I left St Anthony's when I was sixteen."

Victoria looked sad. "I honestly thought that somebody would want to adopt you as soon as they saw your beautiful face. In fact, in my mind, I was sure of it. Did the nuns not find adoptive parents for any of you?"

"They did find childless couples from time to time," Annie told them. "They usually only wanted one child and I was always with Bella Jones..." She gave the O'Sheas a potted version of her life with Bella, stopping only when she arrived at Bella's death. "After that I was alone, but made good friends at Half Way House, at college and at the hospital. I'm a ten pound pom too," she revealed. "It was an opportunity too good to miss."

"Can you ever forgive me, Anne Marie?" Victoria asked plaintively. "We never forgot you. Dec and I pray for you every night before we go to sleep."

"We were always told we should never look for our birth mothers, because we might not like what we found. I learned a long time ago that the nuns were wrong to give us that advice. When I met Bella's parents, I knew there must always be extreme circumstances for a mother to give up her child. I started to look for you a while ago, but something always got in the way. My friend, David, helped, but we kept hitting brick walls. I know why now. I doubt if we would ever have looked for marriage records in Australia, although our next move would have been to check passenger lists leaving Britain. Maybe I would have found you eventually." She paused to think if she should ask, "Did you ever think of looking for me?"

Victoria shook her head. "Like I said earlier, I thought you would be adopted as soon as somebody saw you. I knew I couldn't ask for you back and I knew I would have to go through the heartache and sorrow of leaving you all over again, not to mention disrupting your new life with adoptive parents. I only hope you can forgive me, forgive us, for keeping you as our secret; our beautiful secret. We didn't even tell Jill and Sean. We thought it better that they shouldn't have the burden of their parents' wrongdoings on their shoulders. Now, I think we were wrong and we intend to put everything right."

Instinctively, Victoria and Annie stood at the same time and walked towards each other. They held each other close and wept happy tears this time while Declan wiped away his own tears as he watched. "I love you, my baby," Victoria whispered.

"I love you too, Mum," Annie said sincerely. She gently broke away in order to hug her father. He took her in his arms and smothered her with kisses. "I love you too, Dad, always and forever."

While they were all three joyously overwhelmed with the love they had rediscovered, there was a gentle knocking on the door. "Come in," Annie called as Jill peeped round to find a happy group of people before her.

"Is everything all right?" she asked warily.

"Everything is fine," her mother said. "Come in and meet your big sister."

"I knew it," Jill cried excitedly. "I knew it! I told Andrew that I thought we were all related in some way and that was before I knew her surname was O'Shea. After that I thought we might be cousins or something. He told me not to be so silly, but I felt the closeness as soon as I met Annie."

"Anne Marie," Victoria insisted.

Annie laughed. "I think my friend Bella gave me the name Annie. I used to kid myself I was named after a literary character and I found out later it was a comic strip character," she said. She looked lovingly at her parents. "For you, Mum and Dad, I shall forever be Anne Marie."

Twenty-five

Annie called David as soon as she returned home after discovering her parents. "You'll never guess what has happened today," she told him excitedly. "I'll give you three guesses."

"You've won the pools," David suggested, "And we can all go on a world cruise."

"Wrong," she sang out.

"You have bought a puppy, a Welsh collie to herd the sheep you count at night in order to get to sleep," he joked.

"Be serious," she scolded. "Wrong again."

"I give up," he conceded. "It could be anything, but I'm dying to know what has made you sound so happy." He took a sharp intake of breath. "No," he declared, "No, I don't believe you!"

"What?" Annie asked. "What?"

"I don't want to say in case it bursts the balloon," David replied. "Tell me, Annie. Please tell me before I pass out. I can hardly breathe."

"I met my parents," she announced. I—met—my—parents!"

David was silent until Annie heard him sobbing. "Oh Annie," he cried. "How wonderful! How did you find them? Have you been doing detective work on your own or did one of the priests come good?"

"None of the above," she told him and she explained as simply as she was able, everything that had happened in the last couple of days. "We had worked out part of the story, hadn't we?" she continued breathlessly. "The bit about Mum's desperation when Dad was missing in action. I had already accepted that she only left me at St Anthony's because she was completely desperate and bereft of hope. She was only nineteen and all alone."

"How did they arrive in Australia after all that?" David asked.

Annie told him about the hospital ship and her mother coming over after the war as a ten pound pom.

"That's incredible," David said, in awe of the whole situation.

"I know," Annie agreed. "Talk about divine intervention. I feel very special, I must say. I'd almost given up on ever finding them."

"I'm so happy for you," David told her. "I can't wait to tell Jason. He has a rehearsal after school today. They are putting on *The Wizard of Oz*. It's very ambitious and I've offered to help with make-up when the time comes."

"Sounds wonderful," Annie said. "I'll go to see it and I'll tell Sarah and Stan so they can take the kids. I'm sure they'll love it."

"They will," David agreed. "Jason will love that you all would like to go to see his production. He's very good, but of course, I'm biased."

Annie laughed. "I'm going to have a big family get-together before Mum and Dad go back to Perth," she told him. "I hope you and Jason will come. You are part of my extended family, after all. I will never forget how you have helped me over the years. You are both very special to me."

"Thanks, Annie," he replied, "And wild horses wouldn't keep us away."

~ * ~

A couple of weeks later, Annie was preparing for the biggest party of her life. She employed outside caterers to come into her home and they prepared the best buffet she had ever seen. She had invited Sarah and Stan with their family of four children and made sure there were toys to entertain the little ones in the garden. Along with David and Jason came members of the *Saturday Club* thus named when a select but varied group of people met regularly at numerous locations in Sydney and enjoyed each other's company.

The guests of honour arrived last and were greeted with applause from the discerning crowd. "Thank you, thank you," Declan O'Shea said happily as they stepped onto the patio overlooking the garden. "I am so pleased that my family is complete."

Jill and Andrew stood by, baby Michael fast asleep in his stroller. Annie stood proudly next to her sister and linked her arm through Jill's affectionately. "I don't feel totally complete until I get to meet my little brother, Sean," she told her guests. "But I can wait. He'll be home in a few months and I'm not going anywhere."

Jill released herself from Annie's grip. "Excuse me a moment," she asked. "I left Michael's baby bag in the car. I won't be a minute."

"Do we all have to call you Anne Marie now?" David asked as Jill left the company.

"You do," Victoria insisted. "I gave her that beautiful name and it seems it got lost somewhere along the way." She smiled as she spoke.

"That's my real name," Annie admitted freely. "But if Mum doesn't mind, I'll answer to both Anne Marie and Annie. My best friend in the whole world as I was growing up was Bella Jones. She gave me that name when she was only four years old. She's with the angels now and I would like to keep it as her gift to me. I know she'll be keeping watch on what I do with her legacy." She looked up the heavens. "It's okay, Bella. It's still me down here and I'm not going to forget you."

David interrupted Annie. "I knew Bella Jones and I know she wouldn't expect us to be in the slightest bit sombre on this occasion," he expounded. "Put your happy hat on again, Annie O'Shea...whoops. Sorry Mrs O...Anne Marie O'Shea."

Victoria shook her head at David and laughed. "I don't mind, David," she told him. "I've got my baby back and that's all that matters."

There was a general agreement of "Hear, hear," among the guests and Jill came back as they began to chat among themselves, the atmosphere filled with lively conversations and happy laughter.

Jill stood in the doorway and called out. "Paging Annie!" She paused abruptly. "... paging Anne Marie O'Shea." All eyes turned towards her and a young man who was unable to wait any longer. He ran towards Annie and swept her off her feet, literally, swinging her round and round and shouting, "Hello, big sister. I'm your little brother!"

When he eventually put her down on the ground again, Annie held his hand and said, "I don't believe this. How did you know to come home now?"

"We have loving parents," Sean told her. "They wired me the fare to get home as soon as possible for a family emergency. I thought somebody was dying. They didn't tell me I was coming home to meet my sister."

Annie laughed. "What a shock for you," she joked, "but watch your step, little brother, because I have age and seniority on my side."

Sean hugged her affectionately and whispered," I'm going to call you Annie. I like it better than Anne Marie."

"Hey, I heard that," Declan told him lightheartedly.

"Okay Dad," Sean capitulated. "I'll call her Anne Marie when you and Mum are around."

The party went with a swing. People circulated, asking questions of Victoria and Declan's life in Perth and finding out what Sean was going to do when he returned to Australia permanently. "You have already graduated, haven't you?" Jason asked.

"Not yet," Sean told him. "I wanted to travel before I settled into university. I would like to do medicine."

"That's wonderful," Jason agreed. "I would imagine travelling after you graduate would interfere with your progress in the medical field."

"Possibly," Sean offered. "Now that I'm home, I think I'll stay. I'm twenty in a few months and ready to commit to my future. I haven't told Mum and Dad yet, but I know they'll be pleased that I've grown up a bit since I've been away."

By eleven o'clock, people were beginning leave and had sensibly ordered cabs for the homeward journeys. Jill and Andrew had left earlier citing their new state of parenthood as a very good reason to be party poopers. The rest of the O'Sheas were the last to leave and when their taxi arrived, Anne Marie walked with them down her drive. "Thank you so much for making my world a much happier place," she told them as they hugged and kissed goodnight.

"You have made our family complete," Victoria told her. "God moves in mysterious ways, we know that, but we have to be the luckiest people on earth. Goodnight, my darling girl. We'll see you tomorrow."

Declan hugged Annie warmly. "Goodnight, darlin'. Your mum and I are seriously thinking of selling up in Perth and coming to live over here. We need to be near the whole family."

"That would be brilliant and there's an excellent medical school for Sean when he gets over his wanderlust," she responded.

Sean was listening in. "That might be sooner than you think," he announced. "Watch this space."

Annie waved them off and then strolled back into her home. Wandering through to the deck, she looked at the plates of food on the table, the glasses drained of every last drop of wine and the empty bottles collected and neatly stacked in a corner. *Thanks, David and Jason. Only you two would make sure I wasn't left with all the cleaning up to do myself,* she thought. *I'll put the remaining food in the fridge and the glasses will go in the dishwasher for once. I wouldn't normally put them in there, but there are too many to wash by hand. What an absolutely wonderful evening I've had. My dreams have come true and I think I've found all the magic in my life at one fell swoop.*

She went to bed feeling that she couldn't be any happier if she tried and she had no trouble falling asleep.

~ * ~

She awoke with a start. Somebody was knocking on her door. When she looked at the clock, it was nine-thirty and she had slept right through without stirring. *It must be Mum and Dad,* she thought. *I didn't think they'd be up so early after the late night they had. Ah well...* She adjusted her pyjamas and ran her fingers through her hair before she opened the door.

"Hello, O'Shea."

Annie stood stock-still and stared at the person before her. "What on earth are you doing here?" she asked dumbfounded.

He laughed. "Not that question again. Invite me in and I'll tell you," he said.

Annie opened the door fully and gestured for him to follow her into the living room. He did so without speaking a word and then he took her hand and pulled her into his arms. "I love you, Annie O'Shea."

"But..."

"No buts," he said firmly. "How could I possibly marry somebody else when you brought my heart with you to Sydney, Australia?"

"What?" she shrieked. "Are you serious, Rob Jones?"

Rob took her hands in his while he spoke. "Only one person could make me leave an excellent job, apply for an equally excellent job in a country I have only ever seen in an atlas, pack up all my worldly goods and fly to the other side of the world. That person is you, Annie O'Shea." He dropped to one knee. "I love you. Will you marry me?"

Annie pulled him up and into her arms. They kissed with all the passion for each other they had kept stored in their hearts since they parted. "Yes, I'll marry you, Mr Jones," she answered smiling. "On one condition..."

"Oh dear. Are we setting up a pre-nup already, my love?" he asked.

"...on the condition you will allow me to sign over half this house to you."

Rob held her close and kissed her again. "Just bring me the documents," he told her as he picked her up and swung her round in happy abandonment.

When he put her down again, Annie took his hand and led him to the bedroom. "I have so much to tell you..."

"Later, darling. Later."

Meet Vera Berry Burrows

Vera Berry Burrows is a UK born former teacher living in Queensland, Australia with her retired journalist husband, Alan. She has a son and two grandsons living in Bolton, England. She began writing as a hobby having retired from teaching after thirty-one years in the profession. Since then she has continued to write for pleasure and delights in endeavoring to provide her readers with engaging characters interacting to create remarkable storylines. *Dare to Dream* is her sixth published novel.

Other Works From The Pen Of

Vera Berry Burrows

Tomorrow Never Comes - Relationships seriously affect the lives of a controlling mother, Nell Winston and her rebellious son, Joel until the elusive tomorrows make all the earth-shattering yesterdays worthwhile.

Regarding Kimberley - Kimberley Mason unwittingly unearths a thirty year old dark secret kept by her parents when she forms links with a theatrical agency in Sydney, Australia.

Connections - Connections, for better or worse, made by Jane O'Connell after divorce, completely disrupt her life, both shattering and illuminating her existence with unexpected consequences.

Family Matters - In war-torn Britain, John Hawthorne and his three daughters, Meg, Patty and Abigail, rally forth on the battlefield of their own shattered lives.

My Name is Aphrodite - Rodi Bartlett's worldwide search for her father is relentless, because she knows that somebody, somewhere made her from love.

Letter to Our Readers

Enjoy this book?

You can make a difference

As an independent publisher, Wings ePress, Inc. does not have the financial clout of the large New York Publishers. We can't afford large magazine spreads or subway posters to tell people about our quality books.

But, we do have something much more effective and powerful than ads. We have a large base of loyal readers.

Honest Reviews help bring the attention of new readers to our books.

If you enjoyed this book, we would appreciate it if you would spend a few minutes posting a review on the site where you purchased this book or on the Wings ePress, Inc. webpages at: https://wingsepress.com/

Visit Our Website

For The Full Inventory
Of Quality Books:

Wings ePress.Inc
https://wingsepress.com/

Quality trade paperbacks and downloads
in multiple formats,
in genres ranging from light romantic comedy
to general fiction and horror.
Wings has something for every reader's taste.
Visit the website, then bookmark it.
We add new titles each month!

Wings ePress Inc.

3000 N. Rock Road

Newton, KS   67114

www.ingramcontent.com/pod-product-compliance
Lightning Source LLC
Chambersburg PA
CBHW070304120726
47910CB00007B/2364